FATED MATE PROTECTOR

MOSSY RIDGE SHIFTERS 2

SAMANTHA LEAL

PAMELA AVERY

Fated Mate Protector

Copyright ©2021 by Samantha Leal & Pamela Avery

https://www.totallyromancebooks.com/samantha-leal

Join the Totally Romance Facebook Group!

CONTENTS

CHAPTER 1

*M*ike woke from a dead sleep at 4am alert and ready to go. He blinked a couple of times. There was something out there. *What was it? What woke me up?*

He climbed silently out of bed and drew his shorts up his legs, covering his engorgement. *Still wake up with wood, every day, damnit. Going strong at 40,* he thought to himself with a little smile. His senses were still on high alert but all his shifter instincts told him this was a rescue, not a threat. *There it was again.* It was the smallest sound, but it didn't belong. It was something between a creak and a squeak and it wasn't anything he could identify. His brow furrowed and he crouched down to the ground to see what he could feel at ground level. Was there a scent? A rumble? Animal or mechanical?

His instincts led him to the window closest the driveway, and Mike peered out over the windowsill, still in full crouch. There were times when he remained human, but needed to be closer to the Bear inside, and this was one of those. He was getting the feeling that time was important, and he always trusted his instincts. He needed to find the source of this sound, and fast.

It was outside, at least he'd figured that out. All these years of trusting his instincts and he'd still have a second of panic that he wouldn't figure things out, that he wasn't smart enough. Almost always. He shook his head, *enough of that. Find that sound.* He held his body motionless and listened. *There it was.* The night was still, black and quiet. *Again.* It was definitely a creature. Mike's knowledge of animals was extensive and included all the shifter types from his time traveling, and he still couldn't pick this one out. He knelt to the ground and focused all his senses on locating this creature. *There! By the cars.* He crept closer to the cars in the driveway. Whatever it was, he didn't want to startle it. His size was very threatening to most creatures and he did not want this thing panicking. Mike was the biggest of his brothers, and he'd shot up and out early, so he felt like he'd always been big. He'd learned to handle his size but it definitely had not made his life easy as a kid, especially not in his family. To be biggest was to be toughest, and you had to prove it every single day. *And I am toughest, these boys are pansies,* he let out a small puff of laughter. That puff startled another squeak, and Mike spotted the creature. Well, the eyes of the creature anyhow. Under the farthest car, in the undercarriage, there was a very small set of eyes staring at him.

Mike moved a bit closer, heard another squeak. Usually, the small things were not threatening, but not always. This one did seem especially small though, and Mike moved right in. It was a cat, and maybe even a kitten. Mike nodded to himself. It made sense that he couldn't identify a baby, it was definitely outside his wheelhouse. He peered into the kitten's eyes and gave his best attempt at calming it with a sympathetic Bear growl. This was clearly the wrong decision, as the kitten tried desperately to move away from him. *Damnit.*

Little things are always so scared of me. Mike wasn't sure what was wrong with the kitten, it seemed to be stuck somehow. The noises it was making were hurt sounds, that much he could identify.

He got down on his side, and reached his arm under the chassis of the car. It was a much older model, and there was a lot of hardware around the wheel. It seemed that the kitten had somehow gotten a paw in there, and was unable to get unstuck. Mike was worried that his own hand was going to cause some damage to the kitten, his fingers were bigger than the paws he was trying to untangle. The kitten was on the verge of panic at the sight of Mike's huge hand. Mike couldn't see at all what the kitten might be stuck on or in. Maybe the baby just needed to be lifted out? Mike paused, and decided to just talk out loud to the kitten, since his Bear scared the bejeezus out of it.

"It's okay, bubba, I'm just trying to help you outta there. It's no place for a little baby like you. You need a little cozy spot, a little lovey nest. I can help you, bubba, you just need to grab onto my fingers... Can you do that? Just grab on and I'll get you outta there?"

The kitten almost seemed to understand him, and calmed. It swatted at Mike's big finger. "Yes, baby, that's the way. Just grab on. You can sink your claws in it, I swear I won't get mad and it won't even hurt. Just grab on, I'll get you outta there."

The kitten swiped at his finger again and seemed to sit back, thinking.

"Come on, sugar, you can do it. I swear I won't be hurt, or get mad. Let's just get you outta there. "

The kitten grabbed onto Mike's forefinger with both paws and Mike gave a gentle tug, plucking the kitten out from the undercarriage. The poor little thing clung to his finger while Mike tried to pull his arm back out from under the car without bumping into anything under there. Mike looked at the tiny thing in his hand when he sat up. He felt a little overwhelmed by how small it was, how utterly defenseless it seemed. He looked it over and noticed she was a little girl kitten, and there seemed to be something wrong with her back legs. She was dirty back there, like she'd dragged in some dirt, and he couldn't tell anything without investigating more.

"I don't know what I'm doing, sugar. Let's get inside and I think I've got some tuna or something, and I'll figure this out, okay?"

The kitten curled up in a ball in the center of Mike's palm.

"Dude. I think she's purring!" Mike said excitedly, to no one.

MIKE MOVED AROUND THE KITCHEN WITH THE LITTLE KITTEN held tight to his bare chest. Somehow, he wanted to keep her hearing his heart beat. If he thought about it, he'd have thought it was calming her, but he was acting on instinct. Hearing a mom's heartbeat always soothed babies, he'd heard. Opening a can of tuna with one hand was a little tricky, but after a little awkward manipulation, it got done. He looked down on his baby girl and saw that she was awake and leaning toward the smell of the tuna.

"Good girl, your nose is certainly working! Good girl, Ruby."

Ruby? Okay. I guess she's mine now. Ruby really does fit her. Oh brother. How does one take care of a cat anyhow?

Mike put her down gently next to the plate of tuna and crouched down on the floor while she ate. He could see more clearly now how dirty she was, and that there was something really off about her back legs. He knew absolutely nothing about anatomy, but knew, although she didn't seem to be in pain, that something had to be done. He rolled back to lie on his back and think. Ruby ate contentedly. He needed to get in touch with someone who knew cats. He couldn't exactly call one of the women he knew, he was pretty sure they weren't the type to have cats. They were much more likely to think he was using an innuendo to get into their pants. And, unbelievably, he was completely uninterested in getting into their pants right now. He pulled his phone out of his back pocket. Ruby seemed to be taking a break from the tuna and was on her side, licking her paws and washing her face.

After a little searching, Mike was dialing the number of the local animal rescue. He needed someone to look at Ruby and tell him what to do.

"Hello, Jewel's Rescue. How can I help you? It's a little early, you know." The woman's voice answering the phone really sounded to be on the verge of laughing. Mike couldn't help but smile. He glanced at the clock, 6:03 am.

"Uh, hi there. Oh brother. I'm so sorry. I completely forgot what time it was! I just found a kitten in my driveway and I think something is wrong with her backside. I've never had a kitten before, and I don't really know what to do. I was wondering if you could look at her and give me directions on how to take care of her."

"Oh, sure. You've decided to keep her? You know it's a long-haul thing, right? She's not going to stay little, you know. Do you know anything about animals at all?"

Somehow, the voice was managing to stay non-judgmental. Mike was realizing he might be getting in over his head without feeling any pressure from her. It took skill to make someone think without getting defensive, he knew. He felt really calm to be dealing with a professional.

"I think so. Maybe I, well, I definitely need some tips. I

think Ruby is okay, but there really is something weird about her back legs. When can I bring her in? Where are you located?"

"Ruby? You've named her?"

"Yeah, it just came to me, it was just right for her. She's a little bitty sparkling ruby. I'm a tough guy, I swear, but that's her name," he said with a gruff laugh. Mike could hear himself getting defensive now.

The voice laughed. "No worries. I'm completely sure you are a tough guy. I was surprised, that's all. Your voice *is* really deep and brawny. I was picturing a mountain of a man holding an itty-bitty thing. Ruby fits the dream. I named this place Jewel's Rescue because that's how I think of the animals I help, as jewels. Jewels in the rough, sometimes, but jewels. My name is Sandy, by the way."

Mike couldn't help but smile. This Sandy's voice was drawing him right in. He could feel the warmth of her radiating through the phone line. He felt like he already knew her.

"I'm Mike, Mike Lawson. How can I get her to you, Sandy?"

"Well, the shelter is actually in the process of getting stuck in zoning right now. It's better if I come to you. That okay? If you just get a Tupperware of nice warm water going, I can help you wash Ruby and see what's going on with her backside, okay? You free right now or …?"

"You want to come to my house? Is that safe for you? Do you always go to strangers' houses?" Mike knew he was safe, of course, but Sandy didn't. Didn't she protect herself?

Sandy laughed. "Well, if you are a psycho, calling an animal rescue at six in the morning to ask about a baby kitten, then you are one of those brilliant ones, and I'm already screwed." She sighed. "No, I don't usually go to strange men's houses, Mike, but I do trust my instincts, and since you named your baby, I know you are a good egg. Don't worry, though; I'll bring my knife just in case, okay?"

Mike could hear her bubbling joy. It was so damn infectious! *Who the hell was this woman?*

"Okay, okay, Miss Sandy. I'll give you my address. But don't bring a knife, you're safe with me."

Mike was pretty astonished at the pride and longing he felt when he said that. They signed off and Mike realized he was lying on his kitchen floor, smiling like a crazy person. He was a natural-born protector, all the Lawsons were, but it wasn't like he broadcast it, usually. He couldn't wait to meet this woman.

Ruby had fallen asleep by the tuna plate, after eating half a can. Mike was pretty amazed that she could pack that much in her tiny frame. He picked her little body up and put her against his chest, got up and went into his room to get dressed.

CHAPTER 2

Sandy put down the phone and felt her cheeks. They were on fire and aching a little from all the smiling she had been doing. *What was that about?* Even before she picked up the phone, she'd been smiling at the luck to get a phone call at six about animal rescuing. She loved her job, or her almost job, and seriously was flooded with joy and thanks anytime that phone rang. She'd been up doing yoga before the kids woke up, a daily ritual. Maybe her cheeks were hot from the yoga? She smiled again, nope, that was all Mike. She shook her head, *sheesh, just from a voice on the phone?* She'd been single for too long, evidently. Now she was getting the rush from a stranger on the phone.

She left a note for the kids, Jackson and Cassy. They were used to her going off on rescues while they were asleep, they could get to the bus just fine. They were teenagers, well, almost, for Cassy. Fourteen and twelve-and-a-half, they knew what to do. The note gave directions for the day, and an explanation, and she signed off with a flood of x's and o's and headed off to Mike's.

* * *

IT WAS ON THE OTHER SIDE OF TOWN, BUT MOSSY RIDGE WAS small, so she was there in fifteen minutes. She walked up to the door with a skip in her step, she couldn't wait to see the face behind the voice. It was probably a skinny little guy with tattoos and a guitar rack on the back wall, voice deep from all the cigarettes and late nights. That was fine, but would definitely not be as exciting as the lumberjack she'd pictured. She had no idea what was driving her imagination in that direction, but she was really hoping she was right. She was teeny tiny, and always fantasized about a big guy who could make her feel completely wrapped up in safety.

The door opened, and Sandy was literally struck down. She stumbled back a step and would have fallen down the steps if Mike hadn't caught her elbow. She looked up into the face of this mountain and caught his sparkling black eyes. *Oh my god, he's everything I could have imagined.* Sandy laughed nervously.

"Mike? I hope?" She put her hand on her elbow where he'd released her and felt the heat still, where her body had reacted to his touch. He was enormous. Black sparkling eyes, kind ones. Sandy knew eyes, could read them to see intent, and Mike was kind. How astonishing, because he was bearded, completely jacked in terms of muscles, and what she could see of his arms, covered in tattoos. His shoulders were massive, like *rounded* with muscles. He maybe could bench press cars? *Who had a body like this? Was he a bodybuilder?* Most people would cross the street if they saw him coming. He was wearing a t-shirt and jeans and filled them to bursting. She wondered if he could even shop at regular people stores. *He must be 6′4,* she thought.

The mountain laughed. It was a sound that filled Sandy with a burbling joy and made her smile instinctually.

"Yes. I'm Mike. You must be Sandy. You are exactly what I imagined, you shiny little thing. Come on in, come meet Ruby." Mike led her through a hallway to the back of the house, where Sandy found Ruby asleep in a towel nest on the sofa, surrounded by pillows.

"I was a little afraid she'd fall off, so that's why the pillows. I don't know if she's like a human baby and rolls and stuff? I mean, it wouldn't make sense for an animal but I just didn't know, so…pillows, everywhere."

Sandy looked up him, a twinkle in her eye. "You have the right instinct, mountain man. She wouldn't roll, no, but at least it contains her, if she did wake up, it would take her a few minutes to get out of this nest."

"Mountain man?" Mike chuckled. "Well, it suits. And it's better than what I'm called by most people who see me for the first time. I am a little shocking, I think. I'm happy for you to call me mountain man, Sandy. I'm not sure you can bill me at that name though."

Sandy hadn't stopped smiling yet. This was going to end up hurting her face. *Why am I so at home with this guy? Mountain man? Really? I said that out loud?* She looked down at Ruby, "Okay, I'm going to wake her up, maybe, but I need to get her cleaned up so I can look at her legs, okay? I promise I'll be gentle." Sandy scooped Ruby up and headed to the kitchen island where she had spotted the waiting container of water.

"Okay, Mike, I'm just going to dunk her backside in, see if I can get the gunk off in one swoop. She is not going to like that, so you come over here and talk to her. She clearly is in love with you, to let you save her, okay?"

The look in Mike's eyes was incredible. He looked like a baby, full of incredulity. "You think she loves me? Me?"

Oh my god, this guy! How can he be so adorable and so damn hot?! He's in love with a kitten! He's like a freaking poster!

Sandy cleared her throat. "Yes, mountain man, she clung to you and you saved her. You think there's a woman alive who doesn't love that? Even a kitty?" She raised her eyebrows at him.

Now it was his turn to clear his throat. "Well, okay, I am a rescuer too, I guess. My brothers really get on me about it. Is she going to be hurt?"

"No, no, I don't think so, cats just don't like water that much in general. It'll depend a little on what's causing her back legs to be funny. Let's just do it, okay? Come over here and watch. Be ready to soothe her if she's mad."

Sandy dunked Ruby's backside in the warm water. Ruby was not pleased and let out a yowl and struggled to get out of Sandy's hands. Sandy was a pro, though, and quickly wiped and massaged the dirt from Ruby's hindquarters.

"Okay, Ruby, go back to your daddy." She handed Ruby over and watched this mountain of a man tuck Ruby into his chest and start whispering loving words to the tiny kitten. It was the most adorable and endearing thing she had ever seen. *Did this guy know how freaking hot he was? Seriously?!* Sandy took a deep breath to keep from getting turned on. She was on a professional visit, goddammit. This was work.

"Okay, let's see what we've got here. Mike, can you put her down on the towel? And keep your hands on her? So she knows she's safe? I'm just going to massage her backside some more, see if I can feel any anomaly or any clear cause of the disfunction."

Mike held Ruby and placed his face down near the kitten. Ruby batted at his beard, and Mike chuckled. Sandy found herself staring at Mike's face. She could see his lips through the beard when he smiled and they were luscious and full. His eyes were sparkling again and black as night. He looked so damn kind; it was just enthralling to watch him with Ruby. His hands and fingers were bigger than most of Ruby, and he was being so gentle and careful. *I wonder what he's like with humans. As a lover? With those lips?* Sandy thought.

"Hmm, this is weird," she said, her brow furrowed. "I feel like something's been broken somewhere but I'm not sure what…or where. It's not as simple as I'd hoped, I think you'll have to get her to a vet. I can give you a good recommendation, unless you've got someone you use."

Mike was still talking to Ruby, but looking up at her in concern. "Yeah, give me the name, I've never used a vet for a kitten before. Is she going to be okay?" Mike's voice had gone all wavery. Sandy was afraid she had made it worse.

"Oh God, Mike. She's fine! Look at her, she's in love with you. She's not in pain, she's well-fed, she's clean and warm, and she's got her man. It's all any of us can ask for!" Sandy felt a little twinge at her own words, as she certainly did not have what she needed for herself, but work. She was clean and warm at least, even if single forever and ever. This was work. "She'll be better than okay, just take her to a vet to see if they can tell you what's happened and why, so you can find out about treatment, that's all. Now, I've done what I came here to do, do you need anything else?" Sandy set about gathering her bag and coat, looking away from Mike's ridiculously handsome face.

She felt him behind her suddenly, and turned directly into his chest. She barely made it to his pecs. She gasped, startled and stepped back. Mike put his hands on her shoulders and laughed, "Wait, no, no more falling down. I've got you. I'm sorry I startled you, I move quietly for someone my size, I know."

Sandy looked over at Ruby safely in her towel nest and looked up at Mike's smiling face. She couldn't help but smile; he was downright infectious.

"Sandy, I don't know how to even feed Ruby. Can she

keep eating tuna? Every meal? How do cats go to the bathroom? I mean, I've heard they need a box or something? Any box? Do I have to walk her? I don't think I've ever seen anybody walking a cat, I mean, that's crazy right?"

He was almost talking to himself but kept staring at her face and had not let go of her shoulders. He looked a little panicked. Sandy could feel the heat radiating off his body, and his hands on her shoulders were setting off shockwaves of flat-out lust throughout her body. *Come on now! I can't be going crazy over a man putting his hands on me! Come on! Has it been that long?!*

Mike looked at her closely. "Can you help me, Sandy? I am just not prepared for this. I've never had any kind of animal living with me, I don't know what Ruby needs."

Sandy noticed the crinkles around his eyes as he leaned in close and she took a deep breath in of his scent. He smelled like man, like woods and fresh air, and she closed her eyes as she couldn't stop a flood of sexual desire running through her chest and down to her pussy. She was so warm and liquid there, she could feel her pussy swelling. She put her hand out to his chest and felt him take a deep breath of his own. She wondered briefly if he could smell her arousal, but dismissed that quickly. *He's not one of my rescues*, she thought.

She opened her eyes, blinked a few times to ground herself, and stepped out of his arm's reach. "I can definitely help, Mike. Let me just get out of here and we can talk later, okay? I've got your number already, and I might even have some of the supplies you need. I'm around all the time, I'll text you, okay? I'm sure you've got to get off to work, and Ruby will be fine if you leave her for a while. She'll probably sleep most of the morning, really. It's been a big day for her already. Okay? We good?" Sandy grabbed her purse and stood by the door, hand on the knob.

Mike looked a little stunned but smiled, nodded and waved her off.

She went out the door and walked down to the car, feeling a little stunned herself. "Holy shit, holy shit. That guy is *smoking* hot," she said as she climbed into the car.

Mike turned from the window to look at Ruby, his eyes enormous, still looking stunned. *What the hell was that? I just met my Mate, I know that was her!*

He ran his fingers through his jet-black hair and headed over to where Ruby was snuggled in her nest, curled up and sleeping. It was Sandy, huh? He'd smelled her arousal and it had set off a cascade of feelings in him. She was so tiny; he could've tucked her against his chest like Ruby. But so damn curvy. *Oh my god, those curves!* He had fought off his own arousal several times while she was in his house. Even with Ruby nearby, he'd wanted to get his hands on Sandy's body, over and over again. He chuckled to himself, looking at Ruby. Ruby definitely would not mind. She was a cat. He did know enough about cats to assume they weren't overly bothered by the humans around them. He even knew enough that they were *not taken for* walks, but his brain had been overactive in trying to avoid looking at Sandy's body. He'd been so damn nervous.

Ruby opened one eye and stared at him balefully. He

raised his eyebrows at her and laughed outright. She just curled up with her back to him, emphasizing her disdain.

Mike laughed. This was going to be an interesting relationship, having a cat live in his home. He'd never shared his space with anyone. He'd never had someone or something depend on him and him alone for survival, in a long-term way. He'd saved people, yes, but taking care of, providing for, was a whole different ballgame.

He'd had lots of women, well, a fair number, anyway. But he'd never had anyone long-term, and he'd never felt the certainty he felt about Sandy. This was a certainty from his Bear, a 'knowing' that he'd only heard of from other shifters. This woman, this little animal-saving woman with the wild curly brown hair and the curves... She was who he was going to spend his life with, no doubts about it. Now, he just had to convince her of it.

And how will I go about that? Mike thought to himself. It wasn't as if he could just come outright and tell her that he was a shifter and that his animal self had an ironclad instinct that she was to be his mate forevermore. Right? Because that pretty much guaranteed a call to the police and a restraining order. Everyone always believed Mike was a threat, because of his size and appearance. *And, come on, they are not far off. I'm a threat to most.* Mike groaned. He needed to *not* appear threatening to Sandy, it was the only way. Women wanted to be safe, not scared. He needed to woo her, in a very old-fashioned way; slow and steady, calmly. Eventually, he'd have to tell her all about shifting, and everything up to that point had to balance out the chaos that truth could cause. But first, the wooing! Mike hooted and threw his fist in the air. "Let the games begin," he said in a laughing voice. Ruby just looked at him over her shoulder.

Just then, the phone rang. It was his oldest brother, Bill. His oldest brother only called with work-related gigs and had to be answered. He looked over at the clock. Just a bit past seven now, pretty early for a work call. He answered the phone while absent-mindedly rubbing between Ruby's ears. At least this call didn't wake him.

After speaking with Bill, he hung up and headed out.

* * *

"What's up, meathead?"

Mike turned his colossal head toward his baby brother. Mike *was* a meathead. A giant, a neanderthal, a mountain, a muscle head, bouncer, jock, a redwood; he'd been called everything under the sun. He was just over-sized, as he liked to say with his brothers. His brother knew it and knew exactly how much Mike loathed it. He hadn't minded being called mountain man this morning though. Guess it just depended on who was doing the calling. Kurt was sitting outside the coffee shop, as they waited for their oldest brother Bill to arrive.

Kurt laughed, "I'm kidding, Mike, I'm just pulling your leg today. You ready to roll?"

Mike sighed and narrowed his eyes at him. "You planning on keeping it up? You think you can quit it before I whoop your butt?"

Kurt coughed a little nervously, "Yeah, Mike, I can drop it. We'll pick it up another time, okay?"

Mike slapped him on the back, knocking him off balance, just to remind him of how much size really did matter. "All right then. What'd Bill call me out of bed for?" Mike stretched his gigantic frame. He was waiting outside the coffee shop for his brothers. He actually didn't like coffee, much to the upset of everyone who heard that fact. It seemed the whole town had caffeine in the veins. This was The Cup, owned by Harriet and Max, the brother-sister team who seemed to know everything about everything. Harriet had her fingers in all sorts of shifter politics, and Max was a reliable Wolf-shifter tracker that the Bears used regularly. The whole town came through here on any given day. Not liking coffee was just one of the small things that made Mike stand out.

He could hear the popping and cracking of his joints in his first real stretch of the day. He'd been called out by his brothers for a job on the outskirts of town. Thankfully, kind of, he'd been up already with Ruby and Sandy. He was nothing if not reliable, and he'd rolled and been ready in minutes.

He was, by far, the biggest of the four Lawson brothers. Kurt was the youngest, at twenty-five, but the size difference was striking. Rumor had it, there were some uncles that had his build, but they had never been seen, so jokes about his adoption flew fast and furious. He didn't care anymore, but when he was a teen and began to grow, it was a hard time. Despite his beautiful body, he hadn't been a smooth talker in his awkward teens and somehow brought that shyness with him into adulthood. He'd had plenty of lovers since then, but never anyone to keep. The watermelon biceps, the chiseled jaw, the chiseled *everything* made most of the ladies around him swoon. Well, almost all the ladies. He'd definitely smelled Sandy's arousal but she hadn't done a thing about it. In fact, she'd just about pushed him away as she ran out the door.

He was covered in tattoos. There was just something about them. He'd started with a Bear claw on his chest like his brothers, but had continued on where most of them hadn't. It suited his creative side. There was a Dragon to represent the fire and the flight. A water-colored enso to speak to the intersection of breath, mind and creativity. It was more than most of Mossy Ridge could handle, and yet another reason he didn't fit in, not really, not even among his brothers. He loved his brothers, but they vacillated between treating him like a confusing mystery and a paid thug. Oh, they loved him, he knew. But they used him as the muscle for the company, the inherent 'threat' in negotiations, without a word being said. There were times he resented it, but he kept quiet, choosing to keep the peace. In fairness, he *was* a threat. He'd been fighting since he was a kid, as per his dad's teaching, and he was tough and experienced. He knew exactly how to bring a man, or beast, down in the fastest way.

Mike shook his head. *Enough rehashing. Dad just did what he thought he had to. Move on, Mikey.*

Bill and Tim came out of The Cup, coffees in hand. These were his two older brothers. They were very good men, though they had their issues, for sure.

"What's up, guys? Why are we out so early?" Mike climbed into the back of Bill's truck with Kurt and Tim.

"Max let us know he'd scented more Wolf-action on the north side of the hill behind Alice's. It's about a mile from her place, but I want us all in on checking it out." Bill pulled out of town and headed toward Alice's. "We'll be looking for scent, clothing stashes, the regular. We have got to figure out why we've been having this influx. Everything we've been learning is so confusing. Harriet's still not had any luck with the Wolves we've found. They're all 'damaged' in some way. But Max is worried, so I am worried. His old pack was very bad news. It's not something we want to be surprised by."

Max was a Wolf shifter, not a group that Bears usually made friends with. He'd become part of the pack over the years though, after escaping his old pack. Harriet? Well, no one knew exactly the breadth of Harriet's knowledge, but she was part of the Shifter Council, and had her fingers in much of what happened in Mossy Ridge, shifter or not. She definitely had healing powers, but what more than that? No one had the nerve to ask. If Max was worried, they were all worried.

Bill pulled into Alice's driveway as the front door opened. Two almost teens spilled out, brown bag lunches in hand. Alice stood in the doorway with her hand shading her eyes from the morning sun. "I was wondering where you'd gone, Bill. What's up? *All* the Lawson brothers? Is there something I should know?" Her tone was half-joking and half-worried. Kurt, Tim and Mike all stepped back. Alice was Bill's wife, and not to be trifled with, especially if her kids were around. Bill chuckled.

"Alice, we're just checking out a report of a strange scent on the other side of the hill. It's at least a mile from here. We'll change in the back, I just wanted to leave the truck here so we can get out of here after we check it out. There's nothing more than that. I just wanted us all in on it. Max says it's Wolf. That's it, I swear."

Alice squinted at him. "If I find out later you've left something out, there will be hell to pay, Bill. The kids have to catch the bus and they'll be out by themselves on the road. Do I need to go with them?"

"Alice, I swear. It's just a scent. You know I'd never endanger the kids. Look, I'll send Kurt, okay? Kurt, walk out with the kids, would you? Leah, Ryan, you don't mind if Kurt hangs out, right?"

Both kids nodded and laughed as Kurt began whooping and jumping around like a monkey. They walked out the driveway and toward the bus stop down the road.

"I know, Bill, I just can't remember the last time you called all your brothers for a scent-chase. It just feels weird. I've got to go to work, especially since none of you are there. So, get out of here, go do your thing and tell me all about it later. All of it. Okay?"

She walked off the porch and gave Bill a big hug and kiss.

She waved off the other brothers and drove off. She was the manager of the Ursa Development Corporation that the Lawson family owned. The brothers all worked for the company in various ways. Bill was the head of the company, and family. He was the Alpha.

In a sense, they were all Alphas, in their own lives, but when it came to matters of the family, or the business, or shifter engagements, Bill was the undisputed boss, and the three younger brothers had no issues with it. There was no aggression or resentment between the four brothers; it had been that way since they were teens. The teenaged years had been hard on all of them, and their dad had done the best he could with four angry, volatile puberty-wild shifters, without a woman's touch to call on. Their mom had run off when they were young. For Mike, he had been young enough that he didn't have a distinct memory of her, just vague pictures and feelings of comfort. His dad had been extremely tough and had spent an awful lot of time making sure Mike was tough.

He'd been the muscle of the family since he grew into his size. His dad had taken him on trips to fight with drunk locals when he was fifteen. He wanted Mike to know how to handle himself, how to fight with unpredictable opponents. He'd been taken to other shifter communities, to fight other species. Knowing how to fend off a Wolf attack, or an entire pack, was an entirely worthwhile skill. There were times that Mike got tired of fighting, but his dad had made sure to burn that out of him with constant, unending practice. School had never been his strong suit; he graduated high school, but just barely. He'd never wanted to be the leader; he was the fighter, that much he knew.

As far as Ursa Development went, Mike did not volunteer his ideas. He left the smarts to Tim and Bill. He handled the supply side of things— the ordering, the delivery —and he made the bids on the jobs because he knew all the costs involved. He was always ready to ride in a case like this.

The brothers walked back behind Alice's house and into the woods. They disrobed and shifted, one-by-one, into their Bears. Mike was the biggest, even as a Bear. The shimmers where they each shifted lingered in the early morning sun like dew. The four Bears lumbered up the hill and over its crest to the other side. With Alice's house long out of sight, the Bears spread out farther from each other, smelling a wider swathe of the woods.

After about thirty minutes, Tim let out a loud grunt call to his brothers. They all joined him at a spot in a clearing by a small trickle of a stream. Tim shifted back and crouched down by the stream.

"There is a scent here, I need it confirmed by one of you. It's Wolf, and it's fresh. He stood here for a drink in the past twenty-four hours. Bill?"

Bill ambled to the spot and drew in a deep breath. The large black Bear looked piercingly at Tim.

"Okay. That does it. We need to spend the hour seeing if we can track where the Wolf went next. If we can't get a trail from this spot on, in this area, we'll meet back at Alice's and get the word out to the rest of the pack, and I'll call Max. Get on it, guys."

Tim nodded at his three brothers. Everyone knew the scent of a Wolf this close to Mossy Ridge could be a threat. Maybe just to Max, maybe to everyone. The last few Wolves found in the area had been damaged goods, but no one had any clues as to what was happening. Not yet anyhow.

The brothers all went nose down, circling out from the stream. It was a tiny stream, and it had been a wet night. They knew that if Max hadn't found a trail, that their chances were slight. Max had all the motivation to track a former packmate. He still smelled of fear anytime talk of his pack came up, and no one would discount the animal fear of a hunted one. After the agreed upon amount of time, they all wound up back behind Alice's, shifting and dressing in silence. No trail had been found, and it was time to talk to Max and reinforce the nightly patrols in the area. It would mean night work for all of them going forward. They rode back to the office in a quiet truck, making internal adjustments to their expectations of the days ahead.

CHAPTER 4

*S*andy spent the day in a bit of a fog. *A sex-charged pre-pubescent fog*, she chided herself. She couldn't get her mind off the giant kitty-lover from the morning. Mike. Mountain Mike. He was so damn hot, body like a giant Adonis— and he was a puddle of goo over little Ruby. She really couldn't wait to get back there and be around him again. She wanted to get her hands on his beard and tug him down to her. *It has been way too long since I've been with a man,* she thought, *if one morning meeting made me willing to get naked?! But oh man, I am so damn willing.* She had been thinking about what she was going to wear when she brought food and a litter box over later. *Cleavage, definitely cleavage.* She blushed as she made her way through the day's paperwork. Luckily, she could multitask like a pro. Her body was split in two, brains and 'down there'. Her brain was actively involved in work while her body was lathering up for Mike.

She was applying, again, to the zoning board for permits for her animal rescue. Last she heard, they would approve it to take place within her current property *if* she had the space renovated to accommodate sound mitigation on the kennel area. The whole thing was absurd. For whatever reason, there were zero lost or stray dogs in Mossy Ridge, ever. She'd been running her rescue part-time for the better part of a decade, and she'd never once had a dog to rehome or rehabilitate. She had lots of cats; occasionally, an escaped pet bird; some injured wildlife. She had no idea why, but the board was convinced her rescue was going to be a noise nuisance in the neighborhood. The process of getting her home properly zoned to center the rescue here had been going on for years.

She had a guy coming this afternoon to give her a bid on what it would cost to soundproof a room she never used. The 'kennel' was really just her garage, with three large spots for the 'never coming' dogs. It was a totally frivolous expense but the business loan she'd gotten five years ago would cover it if it was at all reasonable. She lived frugally, and the loan had been very useful for things just like this. The rescue was her main job, but luckily, her income was a combination of great choices from her past. She'd grown up scrappy, and had kept her feet on the ground for a long time, making ends meet. Her brain was nimble, and she'd started and sold a few businesses in her early married life. In divorce, she'd gotten half and residuals. She felt pretty damn lucky and also knew she had earned every damn bit of it.

The marriage had been sad and traumatic, but it was over. She'd had the wits to get out and the kids were better off. They were just five and seven when it ended, and she hoped they remembered little from that time. But she'd gone on few dates since then, and she was thirty-nine this year. She had been thinking more and more about men lately; maybe it was the looming 'next birthday', or the last year of her thirties stuff. Maybe she was just done, the reality of life in a small city with two kids and a work life making romance and dating a silly thing to spend time thinking about. Maybe it was really time to put it away. *But this guy, oh my god. Why can't I stop thinking about him? What is going on?* She needed to take a break and focus. It was time for an afternoon break, and she was going to splurge and have someone else make her the drink.

Her phone pinged, and she was looking down at a strange message.

Meet me at The Cup at one, bring the carrier.

It took her a few minutes to put it together that it was Mike. In those couple of minutes, her brain had gone to virology, drug sales, and abduction. She had to get her brain in line, oh my god, the crazy! It had been too long, that's all. She just needed to get back on track; this was work, Mike was work. For all she knew, she was entirely inventing this whole guy. Seeing him again was what she needed. It would sort it all out and get reality involved again.

She gathered what she thought he'd need for Ruby, and headed out to The Cup. She would just have enough time to meet him before she had to get back for the contractor guy.

CHAPTER 5

Mike watched Sandy struggle at the door of the coffee shop for about one millisecond before he was on his feet and stepping in to help. He lifted two large boxes from her arms before he even got sight of her face, flushed with the exertion of dragging all these things from her car to The Cup.

"Sandy! Why didn't you tell me there'd be so much? I could have met you at the rescue!"

Sandy laughed and put her hand on his arm. He felt the burn of her skin on his immediately. Under all those boxes, she was wearing a fitted t-shirt that clung to her breasts just like his hands would. He could easily imagine his face in those breasts, so easily. He couldn't stop looking at them. What was wrong with him?

She pulled him out of his trance, saying, "I'm used to doing for myself, Mike, and I got carried away thinking about Ruby. There's a cat tower in that second box and the carrier is underneath… Way carried away." She muttered the last as she turned toward the counter.

"Hey, Max! Is Harriet here? She asked me to bring the last of that special cat chow over."

Max shook his head and motioned that he'd take it. Sandy hefted the last bag up onto the counter and gave her order at the same time. Max just nodded and took off with the cat food to the back.

Mike watched Sandy's backside as she was ordering. He kept his eyes low and lazy, to keep his interest on the down low. But man, she was hippy, filling out those jeans like the roundest of melons. All he could think of was getting his hands on her hips. He couldn't decide if he wanted his face or his cock on her ass. Her face was still flushed when she turned to him, and he was embarrassed to realize that he wanted to be the reason she was flushed. He wanted nothing more than to turn her whole body red with heat and hormone. She must have seen something in his eyes, because her flush got deeper, and she took a quick breath.

He could feel the arousal in himself, his cock moving of its own will as it grew. He cleared his throat. "Why don't we sit outside? It's a beautiful afternoon, and I'd like to catch some of it before it goes. Sound okay? I'll take these things out and get us a table."

Mike turned and headed out after she nodded at him. He knew he needed the fresh air to calm the beast in him. He was getting close to being very inappropriate in public, and it was just not the way to treat the woman who would be his mate. She deserved better. He had to slow himself down. He had to calm the fuck down, that's what he had to do.

He sat down and looked in the two boxes, one with various pieces of what he could only believe was the 'cat tower' and the other containing a cat carrier and a dozen little cans of food and a small bag of dry food. He and Ruby would be set for a blizzard, he laughed to himself. There was a bag in the carrier with 'LITTER' written in capitals along the side. He'd just leave that one for later. She was really going to have to explain that one. What wild creature would use a box anyhow? Or be inside for that matter? It wasn't exactly typical for a shifter to have a pet, after all. It sort of went against the understanding and value of animal life. He wasn't even sure Ruby would be at the house when he got back. And he understood entirely that it would be *her* choice if she visited him. He really hoped her legs would turn out all right. He had set up a vet appointment, but they couldn't see Ruby for a week; she'd have to stick around for a while to get looked at. He thought for a minute. A tower. What on Earth was a cat tower?

Sandy sat down with a giant mug, smiling at him from across the table. "Did you know that they make the most incredible Chai here? I almost never splurge for a drink here but my god, Max is a genius with the Chai!" Her eyes were wide and then closed as she leaned into her mug to get a sip.

Mike watched her breasts as they crowded each other when she leaned forward. *Oh my god, you dummy! Slow it down!* Mike cleared his throat, sat back in his chair and looked pointedly across the street.

Sandy sat back too, shifting her chair to sit beside Mike rather than across from him. "Let me show you what I've brought you, so you can get home to Ruby and get set up."

She smells like laundry detergent and sunshine, Mike thought. Clean, and substantial, not some mirage of a woman, but a real, live honest-to-goodness woman sitting next to him. Part of him just couldn't believe it. Another part of him was already impatient that he hadn't staked his claim. He knew, he just *knew.* He cleared his throat again, "Okay. What on *Earth* is a cat tower?"

Sandy laughed and cocked an eyebrow at him. "Seriously? Oh baby, you've got a long way to go to be an old cat lady, Mike."

Mike laughed. "I think I'd be the weirdest looking cat lady in Mossy Ridge, that's for damn sure. Definitely the biggest, and hairiest. I'm not exactly low impact," he chuckled again. "Besides, it's entirely up to Ruby if she's going to stay with me or not, I can't decide for her."

Sandy leaned back from him and looked up thoughtfully, "What do you mean?"

Mike picked up Sandy's mug and smelled it. It really did smell wonderful. He'd never ordered anything to drink at The Cup, just assumed it was all coffee. He took a little sip while thinking of how to answer Sandy.

"Wow. That really is delicious. Man, Chai, is it? Huh. I could finally order something at The Cup. It would definitely make Max more comfortable with me. That dude does not trust people who don't drink coffee."

Sandy laughed. "It's true, Max is really straightforward about it. But Chai is my standby, especially if it's not morning. I can't handle more than one cup of coffee and even that has to be weak. I go all wacky-like with too much caffeine. But quit stalling, tell me why Ruby makes the decisions."

Mike looked down at her sitting next to him. "Well, as far as I know, she's a wild creature. My deciding to trap her in my house is unconscionable to me. I will not put anything in a cage, not even a mouse. It is just not right." He held up his hand to forestall her interjection. "I will make my place hospitable and cozy and homey, and if she wants it, she is welcome, but I will never own her or lock her in. I'll be happy if she is still there, and I've got to figure out how to get her a cat-sized door. But she is free to come and go at her leisure."

Sandy looked at him seriously, her brows furrowed. *She is the cutest woman in the history of the world,* he thought. Even without the curves, he wanted her, and soon. He'd really have to rethink the 'go slow' plan. He wasn't at all sure he could do that. He didn't even think he could let her go home after this meeting, much less for all time.

"Em, Sandy, would you like to go out to dinner with me? I mean, like, on a date? Or we could just go now? I mean, go have a real lunch?"

Sandy sat back quickly in her chair. "Oh! I mean, Mike! I … I have a guy coming by the house this afternoon, to give me a quote on some work in the garage, Chuck Morotti. You know him? I've got to get going, actually. I'll talk to you later about the cat stuff, okay? Just take all this home and get it set up as best you can. I'll call later."

Sandy gathered her stuff and went off to her car in quick strides, like she was running the hell away.

"Woah," said Mike. "Women don't usually run away from me."

He looked down at all the cat stuff and thought to himself, *Well, Ruby, here we go. Guess I'm on a giant learning curve today. Ya never know.*

CHAPTER 6

*S*andy really couldn't believe she'd had a full panic at being asked out on a date. She'd basically run away from an incredibly handsome, adorable guy that she was already hot for. *Oh my god, what's the matter with me?* Mike was adorable, smart and a freaking mountain of a man that she already wanted to climb like a tree. *I'm 39, I'm not dead! There's no reason I can't go out on a date!* She shook her head as she drove home. She couldn't believe she was acting like a teenager, running from a boy.

She pulled into the driveway and was followed in by a large pickup truck she recognized as a Morotti's Construction vehicle. She had cut it a lot closer than she thought. It would be nice to get this project underway, she could deal with her need to escape from Mike another time. Another pickup pulled in behind the first, and Sandy had no idea how many men were needed to give a quote but thought two trucks seemed like overkill. Her driveway was packed with work trucks now. The trucks combined were bigger than the garage to be worked on.

She laughed to herself, *men... always compensating.*

Chuck climbed down from the first truck and gave her a wave and a smile. "Sorry I'm a little early, Sandy, just wanted to squeeze the meeting in before I run off to the other sites I'm at today."

"No problem, Chuck. Who'd you bring with you?" Sandy asked, gesturing to the second truck.

"Oh. No one, I thought that was someone for you. Are you getting more than one quote today?" Chuck sounded a little pissed off.

"Uh, not part of the plan, necessarily, let me just check who it is." She looked over at Chuck, "But, you know, I certainly could get a second quote. I mean, it would be good sense, right? Oh…Mike? What are you doing here?"

As Sandy had been speaking, Mike had climbed down from his truck with a clipboard in hand, wearing a baseball cap with the Ursa Development Co. logo on it.

There is a man who can handle a big truck, thought Sandy.

"I'm here to look at your project, Sandy. I heard you say Chuck was coming by this afternoon and knew you'd want a second opinion, so here I am."

Chuck now looked distinctly pissed off. Sandy knew some kind of male pissing contest was happening and just waited it out. It never paid to try to interrupt these things. And she had *no* idea why or how Mike was at her place. *How did he even know where I live?*

"Okay, guys, let me show you the garage I need done. It needs to be completely soundproofed and set up for three dog pens, complete with running water and a very good drainage system in the middle. I've got some plans in the house of other kennels in case that would be helpful."

The two men moved into the garage, taking the same measurements, crowding each other at each corner.

Sandy had no idea what was going on, but the atmosphere was taut, and very uncomfortable. She needed them both to get the hell out of her place. After about twenty minutes of the men trying to muscle each other out of the garage, Sandy cleared her throat.

"Gentlemen, I would appreciate the quotes be in writing, and I'll look over them and get back to you in a day. When can you get them to me?"

Chuck grunted, literally grunted. Sandy could not believe the men were acting like this. "I'll get you the quote by the afternoon. I'll text you. I run a tight ship, Sandy, and we're the best company here in Mossy Ridge, you know it."

Mike laughed. "Sure, Chuck. I'll text you later too, Sandy."

Sandy looked at them both, eyes narrowed, "Bonus points for the man who gets me the quote fastest, gentlemen." No sense in letting the competitive spirit pass her by. Maybe she'd even get the job done before the next Council meeting, and finally get on track with Jewel's Rescue.

Chuck climbed back in his truck and maneuvered out of the driveway around Mike's truck. Mike was still standing by Sandy, waiting for Chuck to leave.

Sandy turned to him, "You want to tell me what all that was about? Why'd you come over here, Mike? Are you really *that* guy? I guess I misread you."

Mike stepped back and looked down at Sandy, slowly-dawning alarm all over his face. "No. No, no. Chuck is known for harassing ladies, Sandy, and giving high quotes and doing shoddy work. It took me a few minutes after you ran away before I realized what name you said. I couldn't let you meet him by yourself, I couldn't. Not knowing what I know about him. What if he tried to pull something and I wasn't here?"

Sandy looked back at him, intently. "You know, I'm used to handling things on my own, Mike. I've even handled bad guys."

"My God, Sandy, but you shouldn't ever have to, don't

you get that? Nobody should ever be able to do that to you, ever, get that? Not for a lousy garage, or for anything." Mike was looking at her like she was the crazy one.

Sandy shook her head. "Okay, mountain man, I hear you. And I hear the noble man in there. I appreciate you coming to my rescue, I do." Sandy thought for a minute. "Are you going to give me a quote or..."

Mike laughed, "Yes, ma'am, if you don't mind me working here, I can get this place fixed up in a week. It's a pretty small job for Ursa but I can pull a couple guys for it and get it done quick. I'll do the supply list and get you a quote before dinner. Speaking of which, will you run away if I ask you out again?"

Sandy laughed, "I've got an out this time, Mike. You work for me now. It would be highly inappropriate for us to go on a date, right? Harassment and all. I'm sorry I ran away, I'm pretty far away from the whole dating scene. I'm not really ready to deal with it yet."

Mike smiled, all the way to his eyes. "It's okay, Sandy, but like I said, this job will only take a week or so, and then... I'm asking again, so get ready."

Sandy smiled, her eyes sparkling. *Isn't this going to be fun!*

CHAPTER 7

*M*ike knew Chuck from town politics. He was an old-timer, one of the old guard of the town that looked down on Ursa Development because it was a Lawson enterprise. It was the classic split between the old folks in town who had their set social order, and the 'newcomers' who made their own social order. The old reputation of his brothers was still in full force when it came to politics in Mossy Ridge. He didn't want Sandy having anything to do with Chuck or the actually deserved reputation of his company. He *also* didn't want Sandy thinking he was some kind of neanderthal, no matter how much he wanted to club her on the head and take her home forever. He knew enough to know that would only cause him problems. He laughed at himself. *My God, I'm already a goner. This woman is all I can think about.*

He was sitting in the back office at Ursa, with a laptop in front of him. He'd just sorted out the supply list for the job and was ready to send out the quote to Sandy. It was definitely on the small side for Ursa Development, but he figured he could get it done in between some of the bigger jobs. He just needed the right guys to give him a hand. He was sure she'd accept his bid but needed it official before he could get the permits lined up. His brother Tim's girlfriend, Monica, was on the Town Council and would get it through quickly. They were getting married soon, and she was definitely in favor of any new businesses in town, so the fact that it was for Jewel's Rescue would put Sandy's job right at the top of the list. He was looking forward to seeing her more often, getting a chance to wear down her resistance, bit by bit. He couldn't think of anything more worthwhile.

Alice poked her head around the corner, "Hey, Mike. Are you putting in for a new job? My email keeps pinging with supply orders..."

"Yeah, Alice, I'm going to do a job for a friend of mine, and wanted to get it done quickly, so she could move on with her zoning problems. Have you heard of Jewel's Rescue? I'm going to redo her garage to get it up to kennel standards, only soundproofed."

Alice cocked an eyebrow at him, "You? Not Ursa? Did you mean to say it like that or do you mean you're doing it solo? It seems like a tiny job, based on your invoices. Who owns Jewel's Rescue? I haven't heard of it before. Did you clear this with anyone?"

Mike raised his eyebrows at that. He took a deep, quick breath. "Uhm, I don't need to *clear* it with anyone, Alice. The numbers are good, I know we're in a lull right now, so I'm going to keep myself and a couple guys busy on a small job. So, no, its not solo. It'll probably be less than a week, but the guys not patrolling at night need something to do to keep busy. Right? Or do you think I should check in with my big brother on what he thinks Little Mikey should be doing with his time?" Mike was almost snarling.

Alice came straight into the room. "Woah, Mike. I am not insulting you, nor did I mean to in any way. I know you don't need to be approved for any work, I really meant, oh god, I don't even know what I meant. I'm mostly scared that you're so mad. I didn't mean anything, and I don't know how to fix it."

Mike exhaled in a puff. "God, Alice. I'm sorry. I'm just... I get way too damn sensitive about my role here sometimes. What the fuck? I must be more tired than I think. I out-macho'd Chuck Morotti today, if you can believe that. I mean, that guy is a walking dick, and I was chest-checking him all over the place."

Alice laughed out loud. "Good god, Mike, you are so damn scary when you are mad. And I love you! What the hell must your enemies feel?! I'm beyond relieved you're just having a stupid man day. Chuck Morotti is a real dick. I've heard nothing but bad news about that guy, especially from women. I'm not surprised he got your back up. You Lawsons don't suffer fools, especially disrespectful ones. So, what's this new job then?"

Mike sighed, "I just need to fix this up for Sandy, Alice. It would help her out, and I've got the know-how, so I just want to get it done. I need her final say-so, but I might get started before I pull the permits, just FYI. I'm going to head over there tonight maybe, if she's okay with that. I need to get the space cleared out so I can get started with real demo tomorrow."

Alice smiled and said in a teasing voice, "Hmm, Sandy, huh? She a pretty one, by any chance? Frustration, macho behavior, rush to work... All signs of something pretty in the works, Mike... Am I right?"

Mike nodded. "Very, very pretty, Alice. And smart, and tough, and very, very sweet. I'm going to work my ass off for the next week, and I'm just going to hope it gets me a dinner, that's all, a dinner. I don't even know who I am right now. I just need to get to the damn dinner."

"Okay, Mike. I've submitted all the orders to the supply house already, stuff will start arriving tomorrow or the next day. Permits will go in tomorrow barring any problems. I don't have to tell you doing any work before permits is not a good idea, right? I know it won't matter, but I have to say it or my head will explode, okay?"

Mike smiled and put his cap on to go out to the truck, his eyes crinkling over his beard. Alice picked up the phone and called her husband Bill, Mike's oldest brother and the Alpha of the Bear Shifters. "Bill, you are never going to guess who's smitten and acting like a fool boy...never..."

CHAPTER 8

Sandy accepted Mike's surprisingly good quote in a text message. It was much less than Morotti's and she'd done some research on Chuck since Mike left and had been pretty grossed out by what she found. There were dozens of complaints about Chuck, mostly from women. Evidently, he disparaged their abilities to make their own choices, asking after the man of the house all the time. There were some veiled accusations of Chuck being 'grabby' when he could be. Mike had been right, and she was extra glad that he had come by. She'd also done some research on Ursa, as it happens, and was laughing as she read the comments from female clients. It sure did seem like Mike was quite popular, and honestly, that he left a lot of his clients wanting more. There were so many reviews.

"Oh my goodness, these Lawson boys…sure have grown up nice and strong." And "Mike moved me, in so many, many ways, ladies. Try him. You'll see." Sandy laughed out loud as she read. "This hot, bearded lumberjack showed up and rescued me in a hot second. I felt like I was in a cheesy romance novel and loved every second of it. Too bad I'm old enough to be his mother."

She could just imagine the reactions of his clients upon seeing him. After all, she'd almost fallen down the stairs when she first saw him. Imagine if he'd been all sweaty and rippling with muscles. She'd have stripped right there on the steps and begged him for sweet, sweet love. *Ha! Was that really true?! Good God! It was, it really was true.*

Sandy laughed to herself and set up making the kids their dinner and checking in on homework projects. They were old enough now to be mostly independent, but she did like checking in regularly. They'd been home since 4, when their bus dropped them off, watching tv and playing video games. She never made them do work right away; she knew they needed a break after a long day of school. So, after dinner was homework and concentration time. No phones, no screens. Not even for her. When she started making dinner, the phone went in the basket by the door. She was down to braless, tank top and a pair of jeans with slippers. Nighttime was on.

When a knock on the door came at 7:30pm, everyone was sitting around the kitchen table, finishing work or in Cassy's case, finishing a drawing of an anime character. They looked at each other quizzically and Jacks said, "Uh, Mom, wanna get the door?"

Sandy laughed and scooted back from the table. She opened the door to find Mike filling the front step with his lumberjack solidity.

"Mike?! What are you doing here?" Sandy almost yelped. Her hands flew to cover her perky nipples.

Jacks and Cassy came up behind her to see what was happening at the door.

Mike just smiled, his eyebrows high, hands wide.

"Uh, I texted you and tried calling but didn't get an

answer, so I figured I'd just come over. I hope it's not too late. I wanted to get a couple hours of cleanup done so I could send guys over tomorrow to get started. Depending on how many guys I have, it might take more than a week, but not by much. I just wanted to get a jump on it."

Sandy could feel her mind shoot right to the kind of jumping that is just for adults, and blushed. *Oh my god, my dirty, dirty mind!*

"Guys, this is Mike Lawson, he's going to be working on turning the garage into a kennel for the dogs we'll never have. He wants to work tonight, in fact. Mike, is it noisy? What exactly are you going to be doing? Oh, forget it, let me just take you out there. It's fine; whatever you want to do, the kids won't be asleep before ten anyhow."

Sandy led Mike to the garage out the front door. Jacks and Cassy came along too. She pulled up the garage door and flipped on the light. Mike looked around speculatively. He walked into and out of every corner, it seemed. Sandy and the kids just watched.

"Okay, I want to get these boxes out and clear the shelves and tools off the wall. Is it okay if I just move stuff out? Where should I put it?" He looked over at Sandy and the kids.

Cassy leaned over to her mom, "Does he know he looks kind of like a Bear? He's gigantic. How many tattoos do you think he has?"

Jackson snickered behind his hand.

"Hey!" Sandy chided her kids. To Mike, she said, "Hmm. Actually, the kids can move that stuff. They've clearly forgotten their manners, and I'm sure they'd *love* to help with the family business. They are good at taking directions, and could use a little work before bed. And it'll get you out of here sooner so you can get back to Ruby. Is she still there?"

Cassy whispered to Jacks, "What do you think *his* girlfriend looks like? Is she a biker chick? Or a sexy tall librarian?"

"Cassy! We can hear you!" said her mother. "Quit this! You and Jacks will do whatever Mike says for the next two hours, okay? I'll go get some water on for tea."

Sandy stalked off into the house, after waving her finger threateningly at her kids.

Mike looked at the two kids in front of him and smiled. "Ruby is a kitten your mom helped me with this morning. No girlfriend, no sexy librarian, and I'm only a Bear on the inside, human on the outside, I swear," he laughed.

Jackson laughed too. Cassy smiled.

"Okay, let's do it. Jacks, you start hauling boxes out to wherever makes sense. If you need a hand, let me know. Cassy, you know how to use a drill at all? No, okay, here, let me show you."

When Sandy walked back out to the garage, Cassy was unscrewing shelving units from the wall, Jacks was covered in dirt and dust from crawling after all the boxes she had piled under the bench, and Mike was standing back, arms wide, telling them both all about his time living in Mossy Ridge as a kid with his brothers. They were all looking very pleased with themselves.

"Okay, break time. I've got tea in the kitchen, no caffeine and lots of honey," said Sandy.

Cassy sputtered, "Bears love honey, right Mike?"

Jackson cracked up from under the bench.

Mike sputtered back, "Bears *love* honey." He laughed, deep and fully, adding a little growling laugh at the end, but he couldn't keep a straight face while doing it.

The kids both cracked up, Jacks actually grabbed his stomach, he was laughing so hard. Sandy watched with wide eyes. It was wonderful to hear and see, Sandy thought. This guy! He got along with her kids. This was freaking unbelievable, and really damn endearing. *Oh god, I think I might be in trouble.*

* * *

SANDY WATCHED MIKE, CASSY, AND JACKS SIT DOWN together around the kitchen island. Mike was just enormous, and took up one entire end. The kids sat on either side of him and they were completely at ease with him, and he with them. Her heart was tender, the kids hadn't been around an adult male for a long time, and she knew they missed their dad. Asshole just didn't care, and that was that. No one talked about him anymore, but she knew there was a blank space, for them, where a man was supposed to be. Not that Mike was filling any such space, but damn, it sure did stir up those feelings, having him sitting there, all easy and content.

Sandy brought out the tea and poured mugs for everyone, nicely sweet. She pulled some cookies down from the cabinet and offered two to everyone.

"Only two, *mamacita?*" said Mike. "Look at how big I am! Just two? Really?"

"Really, ya mug. You're setting an example for children, you know, of sensible eating, choosing carefully what to put in your body before nighttime. You want to have good dreams, don't you? Drink some more tea, mountain man." Sandy laughed, she could feel joy bubbling up in her belly.

The conversation roamed everywhere; the kids had some kind of joke with Mike about Bears and Mike was teasing Jackson about all the ladies at the high school. Sandy found herself getting a little overwhelmed by how lovely it was to have a man here, and clearly, a good one. *Who the hell is this guy?* Mike caught her eye right as she was feeling so overwhelmed and cleared his throat, raising his eyebrows at her.

She waved him off, and began to clean up cookie plates and mugs.

"Okay, guys, Mike? I'm going to cut the night short here and take your workers from you. Guys, you go get ready to crash, and I'll walk Mike out. Yes, you'll see him again, I think. Right?"

"Yeah, yeah, I'll be here all week; though, with some other guys who probably will be a lot less fun to work with. They don't make fun of me at all. I think I intimidate them with my manly ways. Isn't that nuts?"

Cassy and Jackson cracked up and each punched Mike on the arm as their way of saying goodnight. They were both smiling as they headed out. Sandy grabbed a sweater and pulled it on as she and Mike headed out the front door.

"You okay, Sandy? You started to look upset there for a minute," Mike said as they stepped down the front stairs.

"Oh yeah, I'm fine, Mike, I just haven't seen the kids with a man since their dad, and that was a long time ago. I guess I didn't realize how much they might miss it. Or how much I've missed it. It caught me off guard a little, the sweetness of it. You were very sweet with them. Thank you for all of that." She smiled up at him as they reached the side of his truck. She wanted to touch his face so damn much. *Oh my god.*

"Sandy, you have really good kids. I mean it, they are funny, and smart, and can actually follow directions. Cassy worked that drill like a pro once I showed her how, and Jackson was working like a champ. He wouldn't stop. I know you might not know this, but you're doing an amazing job. You really are. And you're stinking unbelievably fucking gorgeous on top of it all." He put his key in the door, and rested his hand on her shoulder, pulling her closer. She could feel the heat emanating from him right through her skin.

Sandy laughed and put her hand on his chest, "The honey

must be getting to you, Bear guy. It's been a hell of a long time since anyone called *me* gorgeous."

"Well, that'll *never* happen again." Mike pulled Sandy tight into a hug against his chest. "I'm going to tell you right now how damn hot you are, and then I'm going to tell you again tomorrow, and the next day, and the next… I couldn't stop looking at you in that damn tank top. Holy shit, Sandy. You are so damn delicious, I want to nibble you from nip to bottom, and I'm going to hold you tight, right now, so you can't run away from me. First, though, before I lose my ever-lovin' mind, I'm going to kiss you, if you'll let me…"

He released his hold on her and Sandy stepped back, looking a little lost. She took a deep breath and stepped back toward him.

"Kiss me or I'll start screaming, Mountain Man. I swear it."

Mike chuckled and didn't lose a second. He leaned down and grabbed her full bottom lip with his teeth. She could feel him smiling as he teased her. She leaned into his kiss, rising up on her tiptoes and putting her arms around his neck. He let go of her lip and touched her lips gently with his tongue. Sandy laughed. She was having none of this gentle kissing stuff, and dove deep, exploring him with her tongue, nipping at his lips and pulling on his neck to get him closer and deeper. She felt his breath catch, just as she caught hers. *Oh my*, she thought. Then thought went away. She tangled her fingers in the soft hair at the nape of his neck, and Mike reached under her ass and lifted her whole body to his chest. Her legs went around his waist. Her skin was on fire, she could feel her nipples pushing out against her shirt and her pussy was full of molten liquid. She didn't trust herself to speak and wanted him inside of her, already. She ground her pussy against the bulge in his jeans.

He took a deep breath.

She was in Mike's arms, her body at his waist, her legs around his back, hidden from the house but not from the neighbors. "In the garage, Mike, we have to get off the street, now."

He grunted, grabbed his key out of the door of his truck, and carried her swiftly to the still open but dark garage. Her head was tucked into his chest; his smell was everywhere. Her face was immersed in his beard, she could smell his shampoo. Sandy kept her fingers running through the hair at his neck. She was utterly fixated. He could have carried her to the top of a volcano for all she cared. He stepped into the garage. She could feel him looking around. "Put me on the bench, Mike." He took two more steps and she felt him place her down gingerly on the old work bench.

He pulled away to shut the door to the garage. It was quite dark when he turned back, and her senses piqued as she tried to make him out in the darkness. She could smell him, which surprised her. Clean, strong man. "Can you find me?" she asked. He answered by pulling her to the edge of the bench, her pussy pressing against his hottest spot. "Lock the door to the house," Sandy panted. He looked at her strangely. "No kids, no surprises."

"Ahh…" He stepped over, turned the lock and returned. It was a matter of seconds, and Sandy still missed his touch. Coming back, he put his arms along her thighs, his hands at her back, his face into her cleavage. Sandy held him tight as he nuzzled her breasts. "I can't go very slow, Sandy, I've been wanting to lick your nipples all night." His voice was muffled as he pulled her tank top down, releasing her breasts into his hands.

She heard him moan as he flicked her nipples with his thumbs and then lean down to take them in his mouth at once, his hands pushing the nipples together into his hot mouth.

Heat shot all through her body, she could feel her toes curl and her knees rising higher on Mike's body, angling her pussy to rub more specifically on his cock. Her back arched and gave him better access to her breasts. Her hands went back behind her, supporting her torso as he licked and suckled at her chest. "Thank god you cleaned off this bench," she panted.

Mike snorted and rested his head on her breasts as his whole body shook with laughter. He looked up at her, smiling, and then his eyes narrowed devilishly.

"If you can still speak, I'm not working quite hard enough." He lifted her from the bench, sliding his hands up her back, laying her flat on her back. He kept one hand flicking her nipple and the other began to undo her jeans. He stepped back and slid them off her hips and all the way down her legs, pulling them off her feet and throwing them over his shoulder into the dark of the garage.

Sandy heard them land and then felt his beard on her thighs. The thrill at the sensation of the curly hair on her prickling skin nearly blew her head off, and then his tongue found the heat and wetness at the center of her. She was still wearing her panties, and they were soaked, and he was sucking on her right through them.

"Oh my god," she said, as she angled herself directly to his mouth. Again, she felt that smile of his through the dark.

"You like this?" he whispered. "You taste like honey, Sandy. I could do this all day, let me just get these panties off you though, and I'll settle in."

She felt his smile again, at her thighs. *This is so goddamned incredible,* she thought, *I can't believe this is happening to me.* She lifted her foot and put it on his shoulder.

"No," Sandy said. Mike froze.

"You need me to stop, Sandy? I...absolutely...whatever you need," Mike stuttered.

"No," said Sandy, "no more tongue. I want the cock. Your cock. It needs to be now." Sandy wished she could see his face in the dark, to see how he was reacting. But she certainly could hear the moan and the unzipping. She felt his hand on her thigh, and felt his other seeking out hers. He guided her hand down to feel his very hot, very large cock. Sandy's eyes went wide and she was thrilled that he couldn't see her face. She smiled a big, fat grin. *Oh my good god. Thank you, thank you, thank you.*

She felt a soft velvety pressure on her pussy as he laid the tip of his cock there. She pushed against it with her pussy, saying, "Please, Mike."

She felt him shudder and push against her folds, sliding into her with ease, as she was so open and so wet for him. *Oh my god, finally.* He fit her so well, and her body just lit up with bliss as he started to move faster.

Sandy had her feet up on his shoulders and he grabbed her ankles as he began to thrust more deeply. She put her hands on her breasts to hold them as he began to pound her back with each thrust. The sensation was so good, she could feel the heat building in her as he went. She felt drops of his sweat land on her belly and felt her pussy begin clutching his cock, urging him deeper and faster. The sounds coming from her were out of her control now; she was moaning and whimpering interchangeably. She felt the pressure mounting and mounting in her belly and lower, a tightening that was taking her breath from her. She felt like a beast, panting for more, more, more.

She threw her head back and swallowed a scream as she came, her body convulsing against him. She felt him start to jerk wildly as he met her orgasm with his own and he fell forward on her, as they both heaved with the exertion. Sandy wrapped her arms and legs around Mike's sweaty body, exhaustedly but still trying to keep him inside her, and nearby. "Oh my god, Mike, I love you. Thank you so much," Sandy laughed breathlessly.

Mike laughed. "Gee, Sandy, I didn't know it was going to be so easy to win your love. I can do it again if it helps…"

Sandy laughed and slapped him playfully on the back. They were both still breathing heavy and slicked with sweat.

"I'm not sure I can go again right away, Mike, but you'll be back in a few hours, right, for the work on the garage?" she bantered playfully, snickering.

"Well, I'm not sure I'll be taking out this bench. I mean, it's got sentimental value now. How could I possibly remove the first place you declared your love for me?"

Sandy snickered and hid her head in his chest. "I got carried away in post-coital bliss, Mike. Don't take it to the bank or anything." She rubbed his back to take the sting out of her words, but deep down, she knew she meant it, sex and love were very different things, and the words and the feelings were not always connected. But that was a conversation for later. Sandy sighed. "Okay, time to get back to real life, honeybunch, let's find my clothes, shall we?"

"Hold on." Mike handed her the clothes after a minute.

"You can see in the dark? How'd you do that?" Sandy asked. She could barely sort out how to get her clothes back on in the darkness, and he'd found them on the floor of the garage.

"I can, uh, kind of see in the dark," Mike said. "It's like I told the kids, I am part Bear." He laughed, mostly to himself.

"Well, hell's bells, I'll happily put out the Bear bait from now on," Sandy chortled. She tried to slap him on the ass but started to fall, as she hadn't quite gotten her jeans all the way up yet. Mike caught her.

"Told you I could see in the dark," he said teasingly. Sandy sighed contentedly, back in his arms and surprised at how damn comfortable this whole thing was.

"Oh, Mike, thanks so much for that. It was really great, really, really. It's not going to be weird or anything when I see you tomorrow, is it?"

"No way, Sandy. I'll be bringing the guys along and I promise, it'll be all work. All I'll do is wink at you, I swear. This is a job, and I want to get it done for you, on time and under budget. It's the company's reputation, not just my hot sex bunny's house."

Sandy snorted, and covered her mouth as laughter exploded from her. She figured the sexual tension release had made her lose her mind, as she erupted in peals of laughter. She had her pants all buttoned up and her tank top set aright, so she was ready to face her life again. *And he'd be back again, and again, for two whole weeks.*

"Can I turn the light on? Light your way out of here? Or can you see your way out in the dark?"

Mike was already opening the garage door to let himself out. He stopped, "I'll see you in a few hours, Sandy. I might not even shower, so I can keep smelling you in my beard. I'll certainly be feeling you still when I see you again. Just in case I don't mention it in front of the guys, you should know it. You just knocked my damn socks off, lady."

Mike turned and walked out to his truck. She could see him now, in the light from the front porch. He was gigantic, and yet not at all scary, and in fact, adorable. She waited until he pulled out of the driveway, and then jumped around wildly, knowing no one could see her.

"Woohooo," she whispered to herself, as she unlocked the door to the house and walked into her well-lit kitchen.

CHAPTER 9

The phone rang for Mike, too early to be good news. He rolled over to grab it from the charger and noticed Ruby looking at him from the side table. "G'morning puss girl, what's up?"

"Why on God's Earth would you be calling me puss girl?" his brother Kurt said into the phone, laughingly. "I don't even know if I am supposed to be offended or not."

Mike laughed. "You caught me greeting Little Ruby, a kitten who is sharing space with me. Unless you would *like* me to call you puss girl. I mean, I certainly can. I'll make sure to tell the guys…"

Kurt laughed, "Nah, I'm good, bro. Glad you've finally got some company. You've been living like a monk for a long damn time. Even if it is a cat."

Mike smiled to himself. If only he was a tale-teller, his brother would blush! But he wasn't. So the sexy bunny would stay private.

"What do you want, Kurt?"

"The vet over the hill called, she's been finding all the food taken from her traps, but nothing in the traps themselves. She's a shifter and she called Max and Harriet, because she thinks something smart is taking the food, and not animal-smart, *shifter-smart."*

Mike waited a beat. "And why does this warrant an early-morning roust?"

"Well," Kurt answered, "Its Bill and Tim. They want everyone up and out to check the traps we've got set up here. I know the rescue in town has some traps set up for cats and that you're working there today, so they wanted you to get a list of where they are, so we can go check those, as well as what we've set up in the past few months. If it's Wolves, they want to know. Max is already out on the prowl again. That guy is very, very uncomfortable lately. He snapped at me when I got my coffee yesterday. He barely ever talks, and he snapped! I nearly crapped my pants!"

Mike blew a breath out his nose, "Kurt, you called me at 5:30 in the morning to get a list of cat traps? The lady who knows where they are won't even be awake for another few hours. You've got to be kidding me, right? And Max? You probably did something to piss Max off, too, that's *my* guess."

Kurt sighed. "They told me to call you, Mike. That's what I did. Now, piss off. I'll see you later, when you get the trap locations, right? Oh, you might be missing guys at the job today, they're out patrolling. Okay, then. Later." Kurt clicked off.

Mike groaned. Now he was awake. Ruby was still staring at him in bed. He growled at her and she hissed at him, clearly not in the mood either. Mike got up, headed to the kitchen to put the kettle on and make his oatmeal. He looked down when Ruby started winding around his bare feet.

"What do you want, peanut?" He looked over at her dishes. Empty. *When did I last fill them? Yesterday, right?* "Okay, Ruby, more of everything, here it comes." He gave her milk and some of the food from Sandy before realizing he still didn't know what or how to prepare a space for Ruby to use the bathroom. He put a half shoe-box down and filled it with the litter. Ruby looked at him balefully. He rubbed his hands through his beard. "Hmm, okay, okay, not good enough for the lady, okay." He slid the box around the corner and into a dark area of the closet. Ruby looked at him with a slight look of satisfaction and almost sashayed into the closet. "Ah, privacy," Mike said.

Ruby was moving around more and more efficiently, though her backside was definitely not 'normal'. The vet who'd found the empty traps was going to look at Ruby next week and find out what the story was there. Mike felt pretty damn content.

He'd had his socks knocked the hell off last night by the woman he *knew* was his mate. His Bear was wild with the need to bite and claim her officially. He was going to see her again shortly, and he liked her so much it was kind of awe-inspiring. He'd never been quite so overwhelmed by a woman, which made sense, as 'mate' was a one-time deal. Once in a lifetime. *Woah.*

He already loved her kids. Cassy was sharp and funny for a pre-teen goofball, and Jackson was a super smart kid, funny and determined. Mike wondered how Jacks did at school with bullies and such, as he was so smart and also, not that big. It was never something Mike had to consider, as he'd been big so early, and his dad had basically forced him to fight at every turn. Maybe he could give him some pointers. He couldn't believe how lucky he was, and felt like he needed to go for a Bear run to get all his joy out. It was the most exhilarating feeling to run wild like that. The power of the Bear was undisputed, and he never had to pretend he was less than the strongest thing around, or 'watch what he said' or solve a problem. He just was.

Mike left Ruby curled up in a sunspot and drove off to

the trail head. He stripped and shifted for his wild run for the next hour. He crashed through undergrowth and caught a fish in the stream. He ripped into the raw coldness with vicious pleasure. As he headed back home, he shifted in a shimmer and ran down the last of the trail naked. He had left his truck at the base and his clothes waited there. There was no one around and he just wanted the power of his body in all its forms on display. He was gigantic, covered in tattoos, with a large Bear claw on his chest, central to it all. Black hair and bushy beard, he was glistening from the exertion of the shift, when he heard a phone ring. He was startled, it was so out of place. He knew it wasn't his, and there were no other cars at the trail head.

Mike looked around, trying to source the sound and realized it was back up the trail, closer to the stream he'd been fishing in earlier in the run. He moved slowly back up the hill, as man. He needed to know the situation before he knew if man or beast was the better option. Why was there a phone ringing in the empty woods?

As he moved up the trail, his instincts began telling him to shift to Bear, that there was danger here. He could swear he smelled Sandy. How could that be? He shifted and moved more quickly up the trail. There was a familiar smell up ahead, but he couldn't quite place it. It was something fishy and something like cinnamon, utterly confounding to the Bear.

He slowed as he came to a turn in the trail; there was a splash ahead and a human yelp. The Bear took silent steps to take in the scene. Absolutely unbelievably, there was Sandy, holding a large metal trap in front of her, on the other side of the stream, looking stone-cold terrified. Mike scanned to see what could be scaring her and growled in rage as he spotted a very large black Wolf standing on a rock about fifty feet from Sandy, growling and looking at her hungrily. Without pause, Mike's Bear ran full steam at the Wolf. Sandy yelped again and fell back on her ass, with the trap on her chest.

The Wolf, upon seeing the Bear, growled menacingly, all the hair on its back standing tall. The two beasts faced off for a tense minute and then the Wolf flung itself at the Bear, landing on the scruff of its back, holding on with its claws and teeth. The Bear reared up, spinning wildly to get the Wolf off its back. The Wolf landed on its feet directly in front of Sandy. Her eyes looked like pie plates as she scrambled back from the Wolf. The Bear took one long step and with a clean swipe at the Wolf with his massive paw, tossed him into the trunk of a tree. The Wolf whimpered and lay still.

The Bear turned and looked long at Sandy, before ambling off down the trail. Sandy stood on wobbling legs and pulled the trap behind her into the brush, after staring at the Wolf to see if it was breathing. She saw it take a breath and she scampered into the trees.

At the same time, the Bear was rushing down the trail, shimmer-shifting as it ran. Mike got dressed and hauled ass to the other end of the trail, rushing to tie his running shoes and pretend he always jogged this way. He bumped into Sandy as she came pelting down the trail, disheveled, dragging the big metal trap. There were clumps of dirt and leaves in the trap and in her hair. She was a huge mess.

"Woah, Sandy! What's the hurry? Oh my god, you're a mess! Are you okay? Did you have an accident? What the heck happened to you in the woods this morning?"

Sandy looked up at him, entirely dazed and confused by his appearance in the woods. "Mike? What the hell are you doing here? Isn't it like six o'clock in the morning? I can't process what I just saw, okay? I need to sit down, in a car, away from nature for a little bit. A car with doors, and locks, and yes, your truck. Let me sit in your truck, okay? Please? I need to decompress, and be safe for a few minutes."

Mike walked her to his truck, glad it was still warm from his wild drive to the trail head. He thought she might be in a little bit of shock, from the fall or from the danger, he wasn't sure. The warmth would help. He helped her up into the truck, took the trap from her clutched hands and put it in the back. He even put an old sweatshirt in her lap, for the extra warmth, and to give her something else to clutch.

He got up in the truck and just looked over at her.

"How can I help, Sandy?" He decided to just wait, wait and see what she needed. She looked so little and so shaken; he was at a loss. He also had to take a few breaths of his own. *What the hell was a Wolf like that doing in their woods? He had to get word to his brothers. And now.* He grabbed his phone and sent a quick text out with his location before looking over at Sandy again. She had her eyes closed and was leaning back against the seat, her hands relaxed in her lap.

He reached over and held one of her hands. "What happened, Sandy?" So much for waiting.

She opened her eyes and looked at him. "I just saw the most absolutely amazing and terrifying thing that I have ever seen in my life, Mike. Both. Amazing and terrifying. I feel like I should be on tv, talking to the news, this is so insane, Mike. I went up to check on the traps, my friend asked me to 'cuz she's been finding weird stuff in Melrose, and I picked up the trap and looked up and... I mean, there was a Wolf the size of my car in front of me. It was, freaking enormous, Mike. And I swear to God, he was going to jump on me and kill me. Like, I don't even doubt it. I could not have gotten away from him."

"Oh my God, Sandy! A Wolf, here?" Mike knew he'd pay for this but he wanted her to keep talking it out, and process it out loud, with him, so she could tackle the adrenaline crash when it came.

"I know! We don't even have dogs here! A Wolf?! And he

was not some soft cuddly thing; he was acting really aggressively toward me. I'm definitely not coming out into the woods anymore without a weapon or a person, I mean, I can't believe I just saw a Wolf in Mossy Ridge! And you know what, Mike?" She turned to him midstream, "That wasn't even the climax of the action. There was a Bear! A giant freaking Bear came crashing from the other side of the stream and kicked the shit out of the Wolf, flipped him right on his ass, looked at me and shuffled the hell off. Can you believe any of this? I saw it, and I think I need a tinfoil hat!"

Mike was gratified to hear the fight had looked like that. His Bear *was* badass. And there certainly was no question who the stronger beast was. The Wolf had landed like a rock. He'd have to leave it to his brothers to recover the body.

"What was the Wolf doing, Sandy? Why did you think he was so threatening?"

"When I think about it, I think he was following me for longer than I knew. I felt off, you know? But it's not like I'd be expecting a goddamned Wolf! I only lay one or two traps out here, most of the cats and things are in town. I just keep track of these two. Couldn't sleep well last night and I..." Sandy blushed and looked at him with lowered eyes. "I just needed to get a walk in, so I figured I'd check 'em. I love this walk. I'm totally pissed that I'm going to be scared now!" She stopped. "What the hell?!" She pointed out the window. A large brown Bear ambled up the path.

"What the freaking hell?" she shouted. "Did you see that, Mike?! Another flipping Bear?! Oh my god!! I've been living in Wild Kingdom and I never knew it?! Did you know we had Bears like this here? I mean, I knew we had Bears but I always figured they were high up in the hills, not where I freaking walk!"

Mike was trying hard not to laugh. He could swear Kurt

had done that on purpose, to show off his Bear form to the lady.

"Okay. Okay. Okay. Mike. Take me home. I just want to go home now. I need a bath. A long, hot bath. Can you take me? We can get my car later, if you don't mind helping me? I don't even want to open the freaking door right here, I mean what's next, alligators?"

At that, Mike did laugh, a long deep laugh that hurt his belly.

Sandy looked at him for a hot second before the sparkles hit her eyes and she laughed too. She laughed until her body shook, and then the laughs turned to tears.

Mike reached over and pulled her to him, tucking her under his arm and into his body. She fit just perfectly.

"It's okay, baby. I'll take you home now. Just take a deep breath. I got you." Mike turned the truck on and drove her home as she settled.

CHAPTER 10

Sandy was tucked up into Mike, tight. He was driving her home because she completely lost her shit. She'd seen some wild animals and lost her ever-loving mind. *Who am I?* Clearly, Mike was a rock star, and she wasn't going to say no to snuggling him in the truck, but the whole lady-who-needs-rescuing thing was going to embarrass her for a long time. She sighed as they pulled into her driveway. She could see the kids in the distance walking to the bus stop and felt an immense relief. Something was totally normal, at least one thing was.

She moved to open the truck door, and Mike was already there, opening it and lifting her out.

"Mike, I can walk, I'm okay, really."

He held onto her anyways, and before she knew it, he was depositing her on her doorstop. He stepped back.

"Sandy, you witnessed a major conflict between two enormous beasts. You felt your life was at risk. It's not small. It's okay to be shaken. I know I didn't need to carry you, but damnit, I just wanted to. I want you to be okay, and safe, and carried, if need be."

Mike brushed his hand through his black beard. Sandy looked at him as she opened her door.

"Will you come in, Mike? I can make us some tea. I'm actually starving, so I might even scramble some eggs. Want some?"

Mike smiled. "I'd love some, Sandy, thank you. I've got to be at work in a few, but since its only fifteen steps from the kitchen, I think I'm good for time. Also, I hear the boss is a pushover, so…"

Sandy laughed. "Yeah, I hear she's easy, too. You don't want to mess that one up." She smiled at him, a twinkling in her eyes.

"Well, some say easy, some say *discerning*," Mike quipped. "I happen to say, fucking absolutely incredible."

Sandy pointed to a chair in the kitchen. "Okay, okay. Yes, I agree, absolutely incredible. And she can make scrambled eggs like nobody's business. Bacon too?"

"Oh God, yes."

Sandy knew it must be the adrenaline crash after a somewhat traumatic event, but she felt entirely giddy that Mike was sitting at the table again; he just belonged there. She turned to the stove to get the eggs going and could feel herself bubbling with joy. *What the hell is this? Joy? For Mike?* She tried to get the sensation under control. *Just make eggs like a normal person, Sandy,* she admonished herself.

She heard Mike moving around behind her and felt him beside her a moment later. "I'm just going to get the tea going, so you can have some while you eat, okay, Sandy? Do you mind?" He grabbed the kettle from beside the stove and filled it, starting the water for the tea. He ran his hand from her shoulder to the small of her back as he moved around her, and Sandy shivered from stem to stern.

One touch. It just took one touch. She kept her eyes on the eggs and checked the bacon under the broiler. She heard

Mike growl at the counter behind her and turned to find him staring at her ass. She felt her lips curl as she asked suggestively, "You hungry, Mike?"

She watched as he put his hands to each side of his plate and begin to stand. Her eyes widened as he adjusted a significant bulge in his pants, while saying, "You'd best be careful you don't burn that bacon, Sandy. I think you should check it again, now."

She looked up at him and felt a definite thrill run through her as she realized just how turned on she was. She felt the liquid heat in her pussy as she bent ever so slowly down to the broiler, arching her back to present him with the best view of her ass as she went.

She felt him behind her, close but not touching…and heard the sound of the oven being turned off.

"Its all off, Sandy, we'll eat it cold." Mike scooped her up. "Tell me where I'm going."

Sandy pointed him down the hall to her room, glad she was a nutcase about making her bed before heading out. *Ridiculous,* she thought, *like Mike cares about a made bed.*

"Nice bed," Mike said, and leaned over to pull all the blankets off in one sweep with his free hand. "I like it made, and I like what I'm going to do to you in every single corner of it." He put her down on the cleared bed, face down.

Sandy turned her head to look at him, this was so damn hot. She looked forward again as she felt him surrounding her, his face in her hair. He was smelling her, kissing the nape of her neck and slowly moving down her body. She was pressed down into the bed, almost pinned. His hands rested on her hips, his fingers went to the waistband and he slid her sweatpants and panties all the way off. His hands cupped and squeezed her bum cheeks, pulling them this way and that. Sandy turned again to look at him. He was intently focused on her bum, and she smiled to herself. It was awesome to have someone be so fixated on her body.

She said, "You have too much clothing on, mountain man. I need that skin."

His eyes were glazed over with lust but he lifted his t-shirt up and over.

Sandy couldn't help a twinge in her pussy at the sight of him. In the light, his massive chest and shoulders, covered in their tattoos, were just incredible. "Its so nice to see you in the light, Mike."

"Believe me, Sandy, I can hardly hold on, it's so nice," Mike mumbled.

She ran her fingers down between her legs to feel her own wetness beneath her.

Mike groaned and stepped back from the bed to take down his running pants. He kicked off his shoes and was suddenly completely naked.

Sandy spun on the bed to lie on her back and look at him. He was fucking spectacular. His cock was swollen and solidly upright, he had a flat muscular stomach, a broad chest covered in black ink. She felt her whole body melting in desire, liquifying while looking at him.

"Please," she said, pushing herself up higher on the bed, to the pillows.

Mike climbed on the bed, holding his body above hers, laying his cock directly between her thighs.

"Please what?" Mike asked, heat radiating from his skin.

"Fuck me, Mike. Fuck me just how you want to," Sandy whispered.

Mike closed his eyes for a moment. "Turn over." His voice was gruff, with barely restrained passion.

Sandy turned over, raising her ass and pussy up to his waiting hands.

He rested the tip of his cock at the opening of her pussy and nudged.

"It is so, so good to see you, Sandy. We're never doing it in the dark again. Ever." With that, he plunged into her pussy, filling her with his hot cock. He nudged still further, as deep as he could go.

Sandy moved forward with each thrust and slid back in time, to add more and more friction to his thrusting.

He held onto her hips as he pounded her, again and again.

Sandy gripped the sheets by her head, feeling her pussy tensing for explosion any minute.

Mike suddenly reached under her and flipped her over. He slid his cock back in before she even knew what she'd missed. "I want to see your face," he said.

He held her pussy flat against his body, her legs straight up his chest, his hands on her upper thighs. "You feel me, Sandy? You feel me?" he said as he slid in and out of her hot, liquid pussy.

Sandy just nodded. This was so hot, having someone so much bigger than she was, was fucking insanely alluring. His cock was filling her so deep, she finally felt filled, whole. She could do this all day. She felt her body start moving on its own, her rhythm matching his as her pussy started coaxing him on.

"Come on, Mike. I want you to lose your goddamned mind. Fuck me more." Sandy could feel her power, and his, as she said the words, and as they penetrated the fog of his brain.

Mike was on the verge, she could tell, and she wanted to watch him as he came, so she wanted to push him further and further to the edge. She reached her hand down to her pussy and ran a finger along his thrusting cock and turned to rubbing her own clit. She watched him noticing her and close his eyes. He got faster and faster, and jerked wildly as he came with a yell, his body collapsing on hers.

Sandy smiled contentedly, his shoulders and back still heaving as he lay atop her. She had her legs and arms wrapped around him and was flooded with a certainty that this one was good. She was so calm in the knowing, so damn certain. She would wait until later for her brain and her reality to set it; for now, it was just so damn lovely. She traced her fingers along his back until she encountered a line of scars. *Well, figures this guy would have some scars.*

She laughed at herself, and Mike looked up at her bemusedly. "What's so funny?"

She tussled his hair and ran her hand around his face, down into his beard. "I'm just silly with contentment, that's all. Don't get a big head about it." She giggled.

Mike raised himself onto his elbows, looking at her. "I need at least ten minutes, Sandy. But if I want a big head, I can certainly get one." He laughed. "And I'm glad you're so content... I really am. Makes me feel as manly as I am. But," he chortled, "content isn't really what I'm going for, and honestly, you haven't even had your turn yet." Mike wiggled his eyebrows at her. "There is a significant job left for me to do, and a real man leaves no work undone."

He lowered himself back down to her skin and began kissing her belly as he inched his way down to her pussy.

When he took her clit into his mouth, Sandy's world exploded.

CHAPTER 11

Mike walked out into the kitchen, leaving Sandy limp and exhausted like a rag doll on the bed. It was one of the most satisfying experiences he had ever had. Her aggression in finishing him was so damn sexy, and there had been nothing he could do to resist her. He found the eggs still in the pan and warmed them up in the microwave. Turning the kettle on and pulling the still warm bacon from the broiler, he plated up some breakfast for them. *What an amazing fucking day, again,* he thought. Here he was, weak-kneed from the sex he'd just had with the woman he wanted to be with for the rest of his life. This tiny little powerhouse of a woman. In some ways, he'd always been drawn to women he'd rescued; there was just something about the dynamic between his size and strength and their weakness. Like, he somehow was necessary for their survival. They needed him.

But Sandy? Sandy was *powerful.* He could feel the power in her in bed, in her fear at the Wolf, all the time. She was this great mom, she was an expert with the animals, she was rocking the rescue, all on her own. *What would it be like if a woman didn't need me?* He shook his head. Ridiculous.

He made up a tray and brought it back into the bedroom. Sandy was still tucked into the corner of the bed; she'd fallen asleep almost immediately after her orgasm. He attributed it both to his skill, and to the traumatic experience she'd had earlier.

He grabbed his phone and sat down to find out the news from his brothers. He leaned over and grabbed a blanket from the floor, covering her as she slept. She sighed and curled up into his side while he looked at the phone. He couldn't help but smile. She was so goddamned cute.

The news from his brothers was troubling. Kurt had scented the Wolf, but the body was gone. Mike couldn't believe it. He knew it hadn't been a death blow, but couldn't believe he hadn't broken that Wolf's back. He growled, and looked quickly down at Sandy. She didn't wake, just rolled over onto her other side, facing away from him. More texts led to more bad news. Max could track the Wolf, and it led from Sandy's house, up to the stream. The Wolf had tracked Sandy. This was very bad news. *What had that Wolf been doing in Mossy Ridge? And what kind of Wolf hunts a fully grown woman?* There were plenty of deer in the hills around Mossy Ridge. The truth was that Mike suspected the Wolf was a shifter. More than suspected. No feral Wolf would hunt a human when there was easier game around. And no feral Wolf could heal a broken back.

Mike sighed. The texts kept coming. The brothers wanted to know about Sandy: what she was doing there; was she a shifter; was she injured; etc. Mike began by answering what he could, telling Sandy's story and re-telling his part in it. As he typed, he began to think it over, what he had scented and noticed as the Bear. Was there anything there that would help? The Wolf had been large, by any standard, but the healing strength it clearly had must be formidable. And its coloring had been strange too. Mike couldn't recall ever seeing a Wolf so black. He couldn't even recall any grey or white on the body, besides the white of its teeth. It was all just odd, and not good. None of it was good. The idea that the Wolf had tracked Sandy was bothering him more and more.

He slid his way back out of the bed while Sandy slept and began pacing in the living room. What could it mean? How could he manage to keep Sandy safe, when he didn't know what was going on? Would the Wolf be back for her? Everything Max had told them about his old pack had been god-awful. What if he was a shifter from there?

Mike couldn't stay here any longer, his anxiety was growing too large to be indoors. But leaving Sandy was now questionable in his mind. He put out a call and got one of the shifters from Ursa to come round and 'work' in the garage. This really set his mind at ease. He could leave, if he knew she was protected.

He walked back into the bedroom and nudged Sandy, smiling, with her cup of tea. She grinned at him groggily.

"I've got to go, sweetcakes. I got called away by the boss. My man Ross is outside in the garage. Ehem… don't think this kind of service is provided by all employees. It is just me, only me. Don't forget it." He looked at her closely.

Sandy guffawed and put her face down in her pillow. "Got it, Mike. Just you." She lifted her blushing head, "Will I see you later?"

Mike put his hand on her bum, "Try and stop me."

He went to the doorway of the room. "I'll be back before dinner, for sure. Can I treat you guys to pizza? I've been craving it for like a week now. Please?"

Sandy smiled. "That sounds divine. See you later, sweet cheeks. I like that… Sweet cheeks."

Mike leaned over and kissed her exposed backside. "Exactly."

CHAPTER 12

*S*andy heard the door of the house close and sighed deeply. She snuggled down into the bed in utter disbelief that she'd had some of the best sex of her life two days in a row. Plus, she'd had a terrifying wilderness encounter first-hand. If she'd gotten a video, she'd be going viral. Wolves? There were Wolves in Mossy Ridge? The whole experience was just mind-blowing, and she wondered about her impressions. The Wolf had been terrifying. She had the weirdest feeling about it, like, it had growled at her, specifically, in some personal way. She'd been around animals, feral or not, her whole life, and was deeply comfortable with them. This animal? She had felt that if it killed her, it was going to be personal. And that was the freakiest thing of all. Not that a Bear had roared in to save her, but that the attack was personal. *How on Earth could that be?*

Sandy just shook her head. She'd learned a long time ago to trust her instincts, especially around animals. If she felt it, it was probably a wise move to believe it. And what she thought about the Bear? If anything, she'd thought that Bear was probably a local, more concerned about territory than about protecting this weak little human. It had been enormous, like Mike, but of course, a Bear.

Mike. Oh boy. Mike was goddamned incredible. He'd eaten her pussy like no one had ever before. She could still feel the way the bristles of his beard had rubbed on her inner thighs, and the way he'd sucked her clit. *Oh my word. Mmhmmm…* Sandy rolled over and grabbed her phone. She shot Mike a text saying, 'Mmmhmmm… thank you again for all the distraction, mountain man.'

She got one back immediately. 'I'm still on your street. Need me to come back and distract you more? It's definitely been over ten minutes.'

Sandy laughed out loud in her bedroom. 'Go to work. I'm still silly content, ya big lug. See you for dinner.'

She rolled out of bed and into the shower, to actually pretend she would have a normal day, no matter how it began.

Half an hour later, Sandy walked out to see Ross in the garage. The only thing now left in there was the old workbench. Ross was a shy, strong-looking young man who kept his eyes down when talking to her. Sandy felt a little like royalty, or something, the way Ross was so retiring and almost overly-respectful. She asked about the bench and Ross said, "The boss said the bench stays. It's practical and fun. Don't know exactly how it's fun but I don't ever argue with Mike. I'm smarter than I look."

Sandy laughed, "His bark is worse than his bite, I think, Ross. But I'm glad the bench is staying. I can see why he thought it was practical." She smiled to herself, "And fun, maybe, too. Well, I'm off to Town Hall to check on the permitting for Jewel's Rescue, so I'll be out for a bit. Do you need anything while I'm out?"

"Uh, ma'am, I'm pretty sure you don't have a car. Boss told me you got in some trouble out in the woods yesterday. Also told me to give you a lift out there when you're ready."

"Oh my god! I'd completely forgotten about the car! Yes, geez, my god, my brain is just ridiculous today. Yes, I would really like a ride, thank you."

Ross drove her out to her car in silence. Sandy didn't mind the quiet as the car was serving as a pretty good reminder of the scary things that happened yesterday. Ross waited until she got into her car and drove off into town before he notified his boss of her whereabouts. "Pretty sure his bite is worse than his bark, ma'am," he whispered to himself.

Sandy drove slowly through town, just being in the woods to get her car for that tiny bit had spooked her a little. Just, Bears and Wolves! She'd been walking all this time so nonchalantly. Geez. She was glad the day was speeding along, she wanted to get her hands on her kids. Somehow, it always felt better to be in their presence, to 'know' they were safe. She had to drive over to have coffee with the vet, to let her know about the empty traps, and boy would she have a story to tell! It would make their monthly coffee meeting zip by. Maybe she'd have something to say about the Wolf, why it could've seemed so 'extra' intense. It was still bothering her, the sense that it was personal.

She'd love to talk to Mike about it; he seemed like he'd be the kind of guy to trust instincts. He was a fighter, right? So, fighters have to use and rely on their instincts. She did wonder some more about those scars on his back. His fighting was a thing of the past, right? It's not like grown men still fought each other. *Right?*

After her coffee with the vet, she was going to have to hit the Town Hall and find out where they were in the zoning process. *Ugh,* she sighed. That damn Travis Smith was the person she had to talk to, and he was a flat-out jerk. She always got the feeling he would take 'favors' from her to get the zoning done faster. It was never anything so bold that she could take him to task; it was just hints, vague suggestions or a raised eyebrow. She thought he was scum, and the only way she could get the damn rescue approved was through him. There was no other way.

The saving grace of the day was there was pizza waiting at the end. The kids, pizza, and Mike.

Mike. What a stud. She smiled to herself as she drove to the vet's office. That guy was something else. He was funny in the way she liked, he was big enough to lean on when she needed to, and he was a godsend in bed. A total dreamboat. She wanted him there for pizza and she wanted him there for bed, and she wanted him there in the morning. *Woah. I wonder what the kids would say about that.* She thought they'd be okay, but it might be worth a conversation with them first, before she had someone stay over. And hell, she'd have to talk to Mike about it too, she wasn't even sure he'd want to take a step like that. What *did* he want, after all? It's not like they'd actually 'dated' or anything; they'd just fallen into bed like teenagers, or like teenagers wanted to. Sandy laughed. *No damn teenagers had guys like Mike show up. Mike probably skipped being a teenaged boy and went from toddler to total hottie in a week. There certainly wasn't anything other than man in there,* she thought.

* * *

SANDY PULLED INTO THE DRIVEWAY AFTER A STUPID, STUPID meeting with an asshole with legs. Travis Smith was getting more and more aggressive with her each time they met. Today, he had left the world of 'vague insinuations' and suggested that they meet for dinner to discuss the zoning requirements. Dinner at his house. 'Friendly-like', he'd said.

Asshole. She'd managed to keep a cool demeanor while stating that she never mixed business and pleasure, ever. Ugh. *Asshole.*

She noticed Jackson at the hoop with a pretty ugly expression on his face but got him to wave at her as she made her way into the house. Teenagers. She expected she'd hear about whatever it was later, or maybe not. Cassy was at the table when she walked through the door.

"Mom, I think Jacks has a bully." Cassy was twirling her hair and chewing gum at the same times. She couldn't have looked any more stereotypical of a pre-teen girl ever. "He says this kid is being mean to him all the time and he keeps trying to avoid him, but now the kid is waiting for him at school every day." Cassy popped a bubble.

Sandy put down her things with a thud. "Okay. Did Jacks tell you about this?"

"Well, he told Miles on the bus, and I listened. So, kind of. He knew I was listening, I mean, so it's no secret or anything."

"Okay, hun. I'll talk to Jacks about it. Thank you for telling me. I'm not sure he would, boys and all, you know. So, really, thank you. I'm going to get showered first, and oh, Mike's bringing pizza for dinner. That okay? Is it all right if Mike's here for dinner? He might stay for a show or some-thing too…"

Cassy wiggled her eyebrows at Sandy. "Mo-om, do you have a boyfriend? Do you like like Mikey?" She wagged her finger at her mother.

"Oh my god, Cassy! Go get your homework started!" Sandy laughed as she headed up to the shower.

What on Earth is going on with Jacks?

Mike pulled into Sandy's driveway after a long and tense day of hunting for the Wolf. The scent had vanished about a mile from where the body had fallen. Not even Max could pick it back up. The brothers were getting more and more frustrated and worried about the repeated Wolf presence in town. At least all the other episodes had ended well, this one though…was a gamechanger. This was no elderly Wolf, not at all. This Wolf had followed Sandy up the trail to the relatively deserted area of the creek, in order to better attack her. Harriet and Max had gone, again, to the shifter council, to see if there was any news about Max's old pack, any hint of what might be going on there.

Jackson was playing basketball. Mike walked over and noticed Jackson's face had a couple extra scratches and what looked like the beginning of a black eye.

"Woah, kid. What happened to you? Has your mom seen that?" Mike could just imagine what Sandy would say. He looked closely as Jackson seemed to wilt before his eyes.

"There's a jerk at school who's been picking on me for ages. Today, I tried to fight back, shoved him before he could shove me? You know? And he just threw me around like a rag doll. I couldn't even touch him. I'm such a freaking loser."

"Hey, hey, Jacks. You're not a loser. Anyone who stands up for himself is a strong person, anyone. If you got beat, it's just cause he has more practice than you, that's literally the only reason. My brothers lost every fight they ever had with me, because I know more, and none of them are losers, not even close. How'd you fight him? What'd you do? I can give you the tips you need, I've been fighting since I was seven."

The two sparred back and forth for the next fifteen minutes or so, until Sandy yelled out the door for Jackson. Mike had seen Jacks improve just in that short time. It was all in knowing what to do, predicting opponents and so on. He was fast on his feet. Jacks would be fine, and they could always practice more.

Mike headed in with Jackson, to Sandy's surprise.

"Hey, mountain man! I didn't know you were here. What were you guys talking about? We still good for pizza?"

Mike nodded. "We shot some hoops, talked about fighting, did a little sparring, we're good. Pizza should arrive in the next ten or so. I figured that was better than my bringing it, would give me more time here before you see how much pizza I can put away. It's not for the faint of heart."

Jackson gave him a nod as he headed up to get started on his homework. He looked relieved. Sandy looked at him quizzically, as she laughed about the pizza, but Mike just nodded back. He didn't want to tell Sandy about Jacks' problems if it was Jacks' place to do so. He hadn't really had a mom but kinda figured boys didn't share those things with them, probably.

Mike walked over to Sandy when he realized both kids

had gone upstairs. He hadn't stopped thinking about her all day. He just wanted to smell her again. He put his head down and sniffed her hair while she was washing dishes. He had his arms around her and could feel her sigh back into him. She was just perfect. She had this little white tank top on again, like the first night, and Mike found himself remembering pulling her breasts out in the garage.

"Excuse u-us…it's just, kids in the kitchen, you know… kids in the house. Get a room, old people." Cassy meandered through with a glass in hand, heading toward the fridge.

Mike let go of Sandy and she smiled down into the sink of dishes. He went over and sat at the table. "Look, Cassy, no hands!" he chuckled.

Cassy nodded. "Thank you very much, old Bear." She sauntered out, with eyebrows raised and gesturing to Mike that she was watching him.

"Why do the kids keep calling you a Bear?" Sandy asked, putting the dishcloth down and joining him at the table.

"Oh, they were ribbing me about what my girlfriend might look like because I'm as big as I am, you know, and I told them I was part Bear and that's why I was so big. All my girlfriends have to be part Bear too." He laughed.

"Oh my. Well, where do sex bunnies fit in that?" Sandy looked at him with one arched eyebrow.

"Ehem. Sex bunnies are for real girlfriends, not Bear girlfriends. I'm definitely part Bear, but all I want is the honeypot." He kept his voice low to avoid any listeners.

Sandy laughed out loud. "Perfect. Bears should definitely get all the honey they can. It does wonders for their coats." Sandy reached across the table and ran her fingers from his lips into his beard. She felt, more than heard, his growl, it was so low. "Ehem. Okay. Sorry, I, good lord, I.. you really do fluster me, you know?" Sandy laughed.

The doorbell rang. Pizza! The kids came clobbering down the stairs. Sandy stared back at Mike as she opened the door. "Mike? This man is carrying six pizzas. Six? Are you kidding me? For the four of us? *Are you serious?*" Jackson whooped.

Mike just shrugged, smiling.

CHAPTER 14

Sandy loved seeing this guy with her kids. She loved the laughing they all did at the table and she loved that Jacks had been able to have guy time with a guy, about guy things. There were definitely times when being the male and the female parent was too tough a job, and she always worried about the kids needing more than she could give. This was just a single moment, she knew, but it was nice, definitely nice, to have it.

She was trying not to take it too seriously. He was great, really great, and she was lucky to have bumped into him, or maybe Ruby was responsible? She laughed out loud. The kids and Mike looked at her. "I was just thinking of Ruby, and it made me laugh. How is she, anyhow?"

"She's great. She is putting up with me just fine. It took me a while to figure out the litter box, you know, and I had a lot of wild energy last night," he gave a subtle slow wink in Sandy's direction, "so I've put in a cat door, too, so she can come and go at her leisure. She hasn't used it yet, but I did show it to her."

"You're so weird, Mike," said Cassy. "How can you be such

a monster and be in love with a tiny kitty? You talk like she's the boss. You said, 'I showed it to her', like she's a person."

Mike looked askance at her, "Several things. One, I am not a monster, don't try to hurt my feelings. Two, big people fall in love just like everybody else. Three, she is not the boss, but neither am I; we're just sharing space, and I want to be respectful of her life, her desires. Animals don't exist just to please humans, you know. They are wild creatures; they belong to themselves, only, unless they choose otherwise. It's true for cats and dogs, and… Bears." Mike made a ridiculous effort to get up from the table as a Bear-like man. He held his hands wide and 'clawed' and approached Cassy's chair, growling.

Cassy cracked up. They all did.

I absolutely adore this guy. How did I get so freaking amazingly lucky that he showed up? I'm completely smitten, I've never even had anything close to this.

Sandy put her hands through her hair, got up from the table and walked into the kitchen. She just needed a minute. She felt a little out of control.

"Hey. Bunny? You okay? I just watched you go from glowing and pleased to really freaked out. What's up? Kids are tucking into the last pizza now. We've got a minute. Wanna tell me?"

Mike put his hands on her shoulders gently.

Holy shit. He's aware of my goddamn feelings? He can sense mood shifts? Is he freaking magic? What the hell is going on?

Sandy looked up at Mike. "I'm getting overwhelmed by how nice this is, Mike. I…just…it's a lot to have a man here, and being so good with my kids, and so easy? And I'm still feeling this morning… It's just a lot, and I've got to feel it."

Mike leaned down to be directly in her line of sight. "Are you happ,y Sandy, is that what this is?"

Sandy sighed. "I am completely smitten, Mike. Completely." She smiled at him.

"I'm all in, Sandy. I've never been more certain of anything in my life. Honestly. You're it for me. I'm done." Mike's voice was hoarse.

Sandy looked up at him with wide eyes.

"I mean it, Sandy. I'm done." He ran his hands through his wild black hair. "I don't know anything, either, more than that. I just know, I'm done. You've got me, for whatever that's worth."

She couldn't believe any of this was happening. She reached up to cradle his face, and pulled him down into a kiss. A simple, sweet kiss. "Okay, my lovely. I hear you and adore you." She laughed. "Now, you need to go… I can only take so much in one day, and I've just filled up and over-flowed. I'm fine, I just need space to…take a bath or something. It's just such a radical change, so fast, you know?"

Mike nodded. "Yeah, I know." He picked her up in a gigantic hug. "I'm going to be here tomorrow and every freaking day you'll let me be here, maybe forever." He put her down. "Okay, I really will be here first thing in the morning," he laughed. "Romance aside, I've got a job to do and I haven't even looked at Ross' work yet. I've gotten distracted by a woman and some pizza. Tomorrow, I'm all business, ma'am, and I'd appreciate you letting me get some gal' darned work done, for once."

Sandy laughed and shoved him out of the kitchen toward the door. "Kids, you piggies, Mike's off, say goodbye."

The kids looked up from the gorging to wave and smile. Mike headed out.

Sandy closed the door and leaned on it, eyes closed. She hugged herself. *Oh my god.*

CHAPTER 15

In the morning, Mike was still smiling. No phone calls from Bill, no animals to rescue. Just a regular old morning with a woman that he loved. *Yep, loved. I mean it, too.* Mike's Bear growled fiercely in agreement. Sandy was his, and he was done looking, and screw all the 'common sense' people who would say it was too fast. He knew. He knew himself, his Bear knew, and that was enough. It was Sandy.

Ruby meowed from the corner of the sofa she had claimed. "I see you, Ruby. I already put the food out, you little tyrant. I'll be back in the evening. Enjoy your day." Ruby meowed again. Mike loved having Ruby here; it was like having a very quiet roommate.

The phone rang. Mike let out a quiet groan. *Almost.* It was Bill; they were going to meet up at The Cup for the day's meeting. He could get there and get back to Sandy's before the kids got on the bus, probably. He'd like to send Jacks off with some last minute tips. He'd gotten the feeling from Jackson that today was the day Jacks was going to try them out, immediate being better in sorting these things out.

Mike drove over to The Cup, still smiling. Ordered a Chai from Max. Walked out to the tables outside to wait. Kurt was the first to arrive. He sat down next to him, and began to talk about the day ahead. Mike wasn't entirely listening but just nodded at what he thought were the right times.

"… and then, the porcupine went right up my nose, Mike." Kurt looked at Mike, who just nodded. "Mike! Hey, Earth to Mike! What are you drinking, anyways?! You drunk or something?"

Mike shook his head to focus a little on his brother. "Nah, of course not. It's Chai. It's delicious. You know how much I hate coffee. Now I have something to drink alongside you crazies. So poor little me doesn't feel left out anymore."

Kurt looked shocked, and actually giggled. "Chai? The mountain of a man, the biggest baller in all of Mossy Ridge… is drinking Chai?! Tell me, fine sir, do you knit now?" He giggled some more.

Mike cuffed him solidly on the side of the head, knocking him right on his ass.

"That's for showing yourself to Sandy yesterday, chump. What on God's Earth were you thinking?" Mike looked down at Kurt.

"Pfft, Mike. I didn't expect anyone but you to be in your truck, man. You'd texted that there was a Wolf attack at the stream on the north side, nothing about a person. I was just ambling up to see what was going on." Kurt got up, brushing himself off. "I didn't know there was a 'Sandy', man. So, who is she? Is she your newest conquest?"

Mike growled. Kurt stepped back. "Woah, dude, woah."

Mike stood up. The air was crackling with tension.

"Mike! Stand down!" Bill stepped between Kurt and Mike. "What the hell did you say to him, Kurt? Mike! Stand. Down."

Mike nodded his head and sat back down.

Kurt's eyes were enormous.

"Bill, I swear to God, I was kidding him about the woman from the Wolf attack yesterday. I suggested she was a conquest. That's all. Was he going to rage on me? For that?" Kurt looked perplexed.

Bill looked between Kurt and Mike. He walked over to Mike. "Anything you need to tell us about Sandy, Mike?"

Mike looked up from his chair, his eyes still glazed over. "She is *mine*," he said in a low growl.

Bill cuffed him immediately across the face… and waited.

Mike shook his head, then his shoulders, in a full body shake-down. He looked up at Bill with eyes wide. "Oh my god, Bill. Did I shift? Here?" He looked down at his clothed body, and looked back up at his brother. "What the hell?"

Bill waved Kurt over and put his hand on Mike's shoulder. "That's my question, Mike. What the hell? You were half-in Bear mode, without a shred of shift. Who the hell is Sandy?"

Mike looked down at his hands. "She's my mate, like, *the* mate. The only one."

Kurt whistled.

Bill sat down beside Mike. "Okay, Mike. It's okay." Bill sighed. "Okay, well, looks like Mike is assigned Sandy's house for the foreseeable future, until he claims her, or she lets him claim her, however it goes with them. Kurt, don't mention Sandy anymore. Put the word out to the men that Mike is on the verge, and if they know what's good for them, they'll give him no reason to tip over."

Kurt looked at Bill as he pulled his phone out of his pocket. "Does everyone get like this? When they find their one? Is this going to happen to me?"

"No, Kurt. It's different for each of us. I guess it's not surprising in Mike, since he is so close to his Bear, in size and all, that he's so close to the edge now. We just have to get them together and uh, finished? I guess. It's a little out of my wheelhouse, as there hasn't been anything like this for a while. I've heard about it, but like, rumors and such.

"We're waiting on Harriet and Max to let us know what they've found out from the Council about the old Wolf pack and if they're on the move. Harriet might have some ideas about Mike, and what to do. She seems to know just about everything. Mike, just go. Go to Sandy's and stay there, okay? I'll be by tonight."

Mike took his Chai, nodded at his brothers and went to his truck. He couldn't believe he'd almost taken his brother out for calling Sandy a conquest. He knew Kurt was just teasing, and if it had been some other lady, it might've been true. It was the first time in his life, or, since puberty, that he'd felt out of control with his Bear, like something wild in him was taking over. Would he hurt someone he loved when he was like this? What about Sandy? What about her kids? His Bear started to growl, deeply. Mike knew he'd never hurt them. His whole life had just pivoted to be about protecting them. His whole life had just changed, and he hadn't even known.

Bill watched Mike leave and looked over at Kurt.

"Holy shit," said Kurt. "I seriously was in danger for a second there, Bill. I felt it. My Bear felt it. I'm not sure Mike knew what he was doing. I don't even know how to feel about that. If Mike got out of control, I'm not sure any of us could stop him. None of us. Not even *all* of us."

CHAPTER 16

"Okay, okay." Sandy walked out from behind the Bouncy Hut, carrying a mewling cat that she'd trapped in the alleyway. "You'll be fine, mister, just let us get you checked out and snipped up and I'll even see if I can get you a steady home, okay? Quit your whining. I swear, you won't even miss what's gone." Sandy chuckled as she loaded up the car.

She'd seen Mike's truck passing by as she drove out this morning, but had just waved as she continued on. She just needed a little time to incorporate this new stuff. It was all so fast. She knew she adored him and flat-out suspected she loved him. It had just been a couple of days. What the hell. *Argh.* She'd gotten the call about the stray behind the Bouncy Hut and had finally scooped this guy up. She was going to drop him off at the vet's later, after they ran some errands together. He was curled up contentedly in the back seat for now. She'd make sure all the windows were open if she left the car, but he'd be fine, she knew. He was a tough young male; he'd survive some time in a crate.

She looked down at her beeping phone and saw that it

was the school. *Huh, that was weird.* She pulled over into a parking lot to get the call. It was Jackson's principal. He'd been in a fight. *A fight?Jackson?* The principal told her that Jackson had broken the other boy's nose. Sandy could not believe it. She turned the car around and headed over to the school.

* * *

LATER THAT DAY, SANDY PULLED INTO HER DRIVEWAY WITH Jackson in the passenger seat. The garage was open, and Mike was working at a bench just outside, cutting lumber it seemed. He was working by himself. Sandy sent Jackson inside. She had a couple of things to say to Mike before she followed. Jackson waved to Mike, ducked his head and sauntered inside.

Sandy got out of the car and went over to Mike, who smiled at her and held open his arms.

"Did you tell my kid to fight, Mike? Did you? Did you know that he just broke some kid's nose at school? Did you know that he just got suspended, Mike? Did you?!" Sandy lost it. She waved her arms at the house, and at Mike. "Who the hell do you think you are? You don't tell a fifteen-year-old kid to aim for the nose, Mike! You're working on the kid's garage, not his fighting form! You didn't think to *ask* his *mom* before you gave him advice on fighting a kid?! Oh my god, man, I could just freaking kill you!"

Sandy didn't give Mike a chance to get in a word; she just turned and walked into the house, slamming the door behind her.

Mike just stood in the driveway, stunned.

* * *

SANDY WAS INFLAMED. SHE SENT JACKSON UP TO HIS ROOM forever, it felt like. They'd talked in the car after leaving the school and she knew all about the bully. She didn't blame Jackson for standing up for himself and even fighting back, but couldn't believe he'd been taught to break a nose, and by Mike. *What the hell. Who teaches a kid to break a nose? What the hell is wrong with this guy?*

She sat in silence with Cassy while she tried to calm down. Cassy knew better than to approach her mom when she was like this. She cut a brownie and put it in front of her mom and left the kitchen. Sandy could hear Mike clattering in the garage, and each time she heard a noise, it infuriated her. She knew she had to calm down before looking at him again. *And I thought there would be three men here, every day! To get this project done on time. Why is it just one guy every day? It's going to take forever. Forever.* She kept finding reasons to get upset again.

She heard a car pull into the driveway and looked out. *Great. Just great.* It was the asshole with legs, just what she needed to make the day utterly perfect. Travis Smith came sauntering up the walkway, stopping to look at Mike working in the garage. Mike didn't seem to notice him, as he was wearing safety headphones as he used the table saw.

When he got to the door, Sandy opened it before he knocked. "Yes, Travis? How can I help you? I'm very surprised you've got the time to make house calls. I understood your job is very, very important," Sandy said with a slightly sarcastic lilt.

"Well, hello, Sandy, I thought I should just come out and see Jewel's Rescue for myself, you know. After all this time, I really figured I should do a little inspection, you know, get my hands dirty."

Ugh. Sandy's skin crawled every time he looked at her. She didn't know if it was entirely rational, but it was one of those instinct things. Can't discount it. She didn't want him in her house. So, she walked out her front door and took him over to see Mike. Maybe if he saw the work being done, he'd shut up and leave, or maybe if he saw a witness around, that would end this charade.

Mike took off the headphones and looked strangely at Sandy. She could almost feel the anger rolling off of him. *Whatever.* He didn't have anything to be angry about. He had gotten her kid suspended.

Travis approached Mike with a swagger. "You got a permit, Mike? For this work? Looks like maybe two days' work, right? You got permission to be here?"

Mike took a step back. "Are you kidding me, Travis? You know I run a tight ship. Every time you've ever tried to check my lines, they've been straight, and you know it. What is up with you?"

"Well, honestly, I'm in a bit of a pickle. My kid had his nose broken at school today."

Sandy heard Mike make a low humming sound, like a growl or something, but ignored it.

Sandy groaned. "Oh my god, Travis, it was *your* son? I am so sorry. Jackson had no excuse at all. He's been suspended. I am so, so sorry. How is he?"

Travis ran a hand through his salt and pepper hair. "Well, he's tough, he's tough, and I told him a broken nose gives a man character, but it's not right, Sandy, and I'm thinking about pressing charges, you know, against Jackson."

Sandy looked at him like he was crazy. "Charges? It was a schoolyard fight, Travis, and your kid was bullying Jackson. He told me all about it this afternoon. Your kid even put him in a trashcan once, in the cafeteria, in front of everyone. I mean, I do not excuse Jackson's actions at all, and breaking his nose is absolutely foolish. But charges? No self-respecting man would bring charges against a kid standing up to a bully."

Travis took two steps closer to Sandy. "You saying I'm not a self-respecting man, Sandy? You want to stake your business on that? Risk the whole thing on insulting me? I think you better watch your high and mighty attitude around me, Sandy. You better change your damn tune."

At that moment, a piece of lumber hit Travis square in the head and he collapsed to the ground. Sandy turned slowly to look at Mike. He was breathing heavily and looked like a bull who'd seen red.

"What the fucking fuck, Mike! What the hell did you just do?" Sandy ran over to Travis to make sure he was alive. She felt for a pulse, found one and grabbed her phone from her back pocket to call an ambulance.

"Get the hell out of here, Mike. I don't want you coming back. I don't want you around my kids. Get out of here!" Sandy was starting to yell.

Mike staggered back.

CHAPTER 17

*M*ike had done his damnedest to drink all the liquor in the town last night. It was the only thing he remembered really. But waking up at home, alone, with Ruby squawking at him from the sofa as he lay on the floor, made sense in a deep, deep way. He was just glad he'd made it home. His Bear had been right at the surface yesterday, and he had been able to keep it down long enough to throw a piece of wood instead of ripping out the throat of that guy threatening Sandy and her kid. He'd been proud, when it came right down to it, that the wood was all he'd thrown.

But none of it was going to matter, at all, if Sandy thought he was some kind of danger to her or the kids. None of it would matter at all.

The phone rang in his apartment, and he just let it ring. Screw his brothers. Screw it all. He was just going to stay here on the floor until his headache subsided, or Sandy forgave him, or maybe until hell froze over, whichever came first. He went back to sleep.

He woke in another half an hour to a knock on the door.

He opened his eyes to see Ruby glaring at him from the sofa, and heard the knock again, accompanied by some yelling by Kurt. He groaned out loud. "Coming, Kurt. Hold on." He pulled himself off the floor and headed to the door. He opened the door and let Kurt follow him back in.

Kurt waved his hand in front of his nose. "Guy, you smell freaking awful. Please go shower. I have to take you over to Bill's this morning, and no, you don't have a choice about it. Shower." Kurt pointed to the bathroom. "I believe I have a little lady I need to meet. Ruby? Where are you, pussycat? Ruby?"

Mike watched Kurt walk around the living room making kissy noises and watched Ruby watching him from her nest on the couch. Mike smirked, and took himself off to the shower.

* * *

WHEN HE CAME OUT, HE WAS SIGNIFICANTLY BETTER-SMELLING and felt more human too. He still felt like a piece of his soul was burned out, but definitely ready to deal with his brothers. He found Kurt on the floor with Ruby, dragging a string along the floor. Ruby was having no part in it, but every once in a while, Kurt rolled onto his back, and Mike swore Ruby looked like she was laughing.

"Ehem, Kurt. Sorry to interrupt your kitty time, but what's up? What are you doing here?" Mike asked.

Kurt rolled again to be on all fours and looked up at Mike. "We gots to go, bro. Bill's got something going on with the Wolves and needs your muscle behind him. Max thinks he's found a den. We need to go in unified, all together, in case it's an *active* den."

Kurt paused. "The thing is, Mike, we need you all in. Like, in control. If you are not in control, or feel like you're going to get lost in the mate stuff, then you get a pass, you can't come. So, I'm really here to ask if you *can* come. Are you good?"

Mike harumphed. "I can kick your ass backwards and forwards. Is that what you're asking me?"

Kurt grimaced and looked down at the floor. "Is your Bear in control or are you? What if someone says the word you can't handle? And I'm sure as hell not going to say it… How much more submissive can I be? I'm literally groveling at your damn feet, Mike. You seriously think I pose a threat? What if someone does? Can you control it? That is what I am asking."

Mike looked down at his brother. He *was* literally on the ground. *What* would *he do if Sandy was in danger right now? What would he do if one of his brothers said her name? Or challenged him about her? Not that she'd ever see him again, anyway; she'd cast him out.* Mike moaned and crumpled down to sit by his brother.

"She's cast me out, Kurt. Cast me out." Mike pulled on his beard. "I don't know if I'm in control, I don't have any idea how to deal with this feeling, at all. My whole body is on point, headed for her, to protect, to love, and a brick house just dropped from the sky on me. How do I live like this?" Mike looked at Kurt pleadingly, "How do I live like this?"

Kurt came over to sit next to his brother. "I love you, Mike, so much. You're going to figure it out. We're going to figure it out, okay? It's going to suck, in the short term, but you'll make it through this. You've got us, always. Okay? We'll just deal with things one day at a time, starting now. Just today. You with me?"

"I want to be, Kurt. I think I need to get out and shift, maybe it'll be easier for everyone if I stay a Bear for a while, the threat level won't be so high. I can be the point man if things go sideways. I've got to at least try, for today, anyhow."

"You got this man, you do. Just for today. We'll deal with other things tomorrow. Just today. Just focus on today. Come on, let's go."

Kurt and Mike got up and headed to the door.

"Wait," said Kurt. He bowed down next to Ruby. "Goodbye, m'lady. Until we meet again." He made kissy noises as he moved away.

Mike laughed out loud at the expression on Ruby's face. He couldn't tell if she scorned him or was mildly in love.

"Good to hear you laugh, man," Kurt said as he slapped his shoulder. They moved out and onto Bill's.

* * *

THERE WAS A LARGE GATHERING ALREADY AT BILL'S BY THE time they arrived. Bill looked at Kurt and Mike, and nodded. He turned to the crowd and told them the plan.

"Okay. Max scented a group. They're based around the old mine shaft on the northern side of Emmet's Hill. Everyone know it?"

The crowd nodded and muttered.

"We know there is one or more shifter Wolves using the mine. We don't know anything more than that, so we are going in with the big guys first. Our job is to incapacitate but not kill. Am I very clear to everyone about that? I know you think your people are in danger, and I get it, believe me. But we are not on a killing mission here. We are gathering information. You have the skills you need to incapacitate, and I demand you use them, as your Alpha. Now, tell me again, Are we *clear*?!"

The group answered loudly in the affirmative.

"Okay. Now, let's go. Stay in contact with others as you move. No one go into the shaft until we're all up there. Go."

With that, there were dozens of shimmers as the men

shifted into their Bear forms, with one exception, Max, who was traveling with them in his Wolf form.

* * *

THE BEARS ARRIVED SILENTLY, WAITING IN A ROUGH SEMI-circle around the mouth of the mine shaft. The Lawson brothers took the lead, with Bill and Kurt heading in first, in Bear form, and Tim and Mike waiting just outside the mine opening, to clip whoever might make it out.

It took only five minutes before Kurt came running out in man form, naked, carrying a preteen girl, holding a gash on her head. *Cassy!*

"Go!" yelled Kurt to Mike. "Go! It's about Sandy!! Get out of here!!"

Mike let out a growl so deep and fierce that the other Bears stepped back. He was already running.

CHAPTER 18

Sandy went to answer the door. It wasn't really all that common to have someone at the door in the morning, or any time, really. She opened it to find a scrawny teenager with a band-aid on his nose.

"Yes?" she asked. He was moving weirdly, she thought, and then she noticed the hunting knife, deadly in his hands. She backed up immediately. He followed her into the house.

"What do you want? My wallet is on the counter. Take it. Take whatever you want. Just get out of here!" Sandy was trying wildly to think of where her phone was. She thought it was upstairs. *There's no way to go upstairs without him following and the kids are up there. No way he's getting near the kids.* She moved back further into the kitchen, maybe she could grab her own knife.

"Jackson!" the boy yelled. *What? He knows my kid? Oh my god, the nose! This is the kid. Fuck.*

"Hey, hey. Don't involve Jackson in this. I can give you whatever you need. I have lots of money, you can take my cards too. I won't report them lost for hours, I swear." Sandy could hear the desperation in her voice and then worse, she heard Jackson on the stairs.

"No, Jacks, don't come down!" Sandy yelled, but it was too late. The scrawny kid hit her across the face and held the knife to her throat as Jackson came slowly around the corner.

"What the hell? Sean? What the hell are you doing to my mom?"

"This is payback, Jacks. You embarrassed me in front of the whole school, man. You fucking broke my nose! You know my dad? He won't let me get it fixed, because it shows a man's character. That bastard. So now I'm going to have a fucked up nose, forever. So, fuck you, dude."

"I broke your nose, you cocksucker. So now you're going to attack my mother?! In what fucked up world is that the same thing?"

"Jackson," Sandy said in a warning tone. "Let's just give Sean what he wants, okay? What do you want, Sean?"

Sean looked at her and laughed. "I don't want anything from you, Sandy. You are for my dad. He's been bothered by you since you started this whole rescue thing. He thinks you're uppity. At least, that's the most recent complaint. I'm bringing you to him."

"What the hell makes you think my mom is going anywhere with you?" Jackson yelled.

Sean let out a low macabre laugh. "If you want Cassy back, you'll both be coming with me, right now. Haven't even noticed she was gone, huh?"

Both Sandy and Jacks were silent. Sandy could feel the blood rushing in her ears. She knew she was either going to pass out or kill this kid with her bare hands. But first, she had to find out about Cassy. She'd assumed she was upstairs! She hadn't wanted to involve her in this! *Oh my god, oh my god, Cassy!*

"Okay, Sean, tell me where Cassy is. I'll go right now. Jackson, you stay here and wait for me to call, okay?"

Sean laughed his sick laugh again. "You think you're in charge here, Sandy? You're both coming with me, and right now. I've got the truck out front. Jackson, come over here, tie your mother's hands together, tight now, and then I'll do yours. We're out of here. I'm driving."

Sandy saw a shadow moving by the side of the house. The front door was still open. She could just hope a neighbor passing by had seen it open and maybe, maybe there was help coming…*Cassy, where was Cassy?* She let Jackson tie her hands in front of her, noticing how gently he did so. *This couldn't be happening.* She could feel him shaking and looking at her questioningly. She had nothing to give him and just whispered, "We'll figure this out, Jacks. We just have to get to Cassy."

Jackson nodded and Sean began to tie his hands behind his back.

"Okay, now, follow me outside. We're done here."

Jackson and Sandy stepped outside the house, Sean followed, a few steps back. They'd gone down the walkway nearly halfway when Sandy felt a large shape behind her. She turned to find a Bear growling at Sean, lying flat on his back, with a giant paw on his chest. A Bear. She looked at Jackson, and they both backed away, slowly, toward the truck.

"Get in the truck," she whispered, and the Bear heard her and turned to look at her.

"Wait," she said. "Jackson, that's the same Bear that attacked the Wolf at the stream. I swear to god. How is that even possible? Wait. Forget it. We've got to find Cassy. Where is…?" She saw the knife on the ground by Sean's head. She scrambled down and picked it up.

"Sean, you tell me, right now, where my daughter is or so help me, I will give you more scars than you can handle. You ever hear of the guy who had loser carved into his forehead? No? I am pretty sure he left town. Yeah, I'd do that. Tell me where my fucking daughter is."

Sandy was crouched down at Sean's side, right next to the Bear. She didn't care anymore; she *had* to find Cassy. The Bear turned its massive head and nudged her, pushed her away from Sean. The Bear looked like it was shaking its head.

"What the fuck, Bear! Where's my fucking daughter!!" Sandy could feel herself losing it. She felt Jackson trying to pull her away from the Bear and Sean.

Sean started to cry, small whimpering cries.

Sandy stepped back to stand with Jackson. She turned away from the Bear. She didn't know what was going to happen but she knew she didn't want to see a Bear eat Sean, if he was the only person who knew where Cassy was.

"Mom, somethings happening," Jackson whispered. Sandy turned to see the air shimmering above the Bear. The Bear was shrinking down, losing its color, from darkest brown to pale, pale skin. *Oh my god.*

Jackson gasped. "Mom! Mom! That's Mike. It's Mike, Mom!"

Sandy could not believe what she had just seen. Could. Not.

Mike was crouched over Sean, naked as a jaybird. She could hear him whispering to Sean, and saw Sean close his eyes and nod.

"Sandy. We've got Cassy already. She's fine. She's fine."

Sandy slumped to the ground with relief. *Cassy is okay. Cassy is okay.*

Jackson had his ropes off and worked at untying her hands as she sat quietly, looking over at Sean. Mike's brothers arrived in the next few moments, and Cassy climbed down and ran to her mother, crying. Kurt handed

Mike some clothes from the truck, and Bill took Sean away to sit quietly and wait for the next steps. His hands were bound now, and Bill had placed a strange sigil on his forehead.

Mike came out of the house, barefoot but dressed now. He walked over to Sandy and sat near her and the kids. Jackson leaped over and into a hug. Sandy shook her head. Jackson hadn't hugged any man in years. Mike just let it happen, and released Jackson with a tussle of his head.

"Is it over, Mike? Is it done? Are we done?" Jackson asked.

Cassy looked up from Sandy's arms. "Did they get the dad? That guy Travis? He's a Wolf, you know, Mom. He was that Wolf at the stream. He was the one who grabbed me, to get you to come. He just was rough, he didn't hurt me at all, Mom, he just wanted you."

Mike growled a little. It made a lot more sense to Sandy now, but she still pulled the kids back to her, as she watched him warily.

Mike put his hands up in a gesture of peace. "I am literally part Bear. I can't stop a growl when I hear a threat to children. I can't and I won't." Mike put his hands down.

"You stopped me from hurting Sean, Mike. I would never have forgiven myself for that. I could have killed him in that moment. I really could have, but I don't think I could have lived with myself, even if it meant getting Cassy back faster. He's just a kid." Sandy put her hand on Mike's forearm. "I don't know what you are or what it means, but I am very grateful for that. Above and beyond stopping Sean, you stopped me. And..." Sandy's voice cracked, "I can't tell you how glad I am that you stopped me." She put her head down on Cassy's and hugged Jackson again.

Jackson leaned away from him mom, while still staying close, and asked Mike, "What about Sean's dad, Mike? Where is he? Is he part of your pack or whatever? Why is he bad? What is he doing? Why did he want my mom?"

Mike growled again. "Travis Smith is a Wolf shifter. He does not belong to any pack. He's been living in town all this time and covering his scent. Constantly, by my guess. I think Sean may have just shifted for the first time, lately, and maybe Travis cracked trying to keep it all under wraps. I don't even know if Travis knew Mossy Ridge is full of shifters. Mostly Bears, but still. My brothers are collecting Travis now. He's not strong enough to evade them, now that they have his false scent. There is no more threat to you or any of your family, Jacks. You have my word."

Jacks nodded and leaned back into his mom.

Sandy sighed a deep sigh. "Okay. Mike, I want to get the kids in the house and maybe figure out if we need food and stuff. Can you stay? I just don't want to have any of us on our own right now. I… Please, could you?"

"Of course, Sandy. You don't even have to ask. I would've camped on the front steps if you hadn't asked me in. I'm not going anywhere until it's done, really done."

Sandy and the kids headed in; Mike followed. "What did Bill put on Sean's forehead, Mike?" asked Cassy.

"It's a sigil that will keep him from changing. Young ones are often more chaotic when they first begin shifting, and he didn't want Sean shifting in the truck on the way to the house."

Mike closed the door behind him, locking it. Sandy looked up at him, curiously. "Sandy, seriously? You don't usually lock your door? For real?"

Sandy grimaced and looked down, "I never had reason, Mike. Never." She sat down heavily on the sofa. The kids headed upstairs, grabbing their phones on the way.

"Hey, guys. No Bear stuff, okay? The world is not ready,"

Mike said. They both nodded. "My friends wouldn't believe me anyway, Mike, not for a second," said Cassy.

"No worries," said Jacks.

Mike came over and sat by her, "Are you okay, Sandy?"

She nodded and leaned into his chest with a sob. "I almost cut a kid, Mike. You are a Bear on the inside, and I'm pretty sure I'm more freaked out by my actions than yours. I don't even know if I can look my own kids in the eyes anymore. I can't believe Jackson saw me like that."

"Sandy! My god, honey, you needed to find out about Cassy! And you didn't actually do anything, Sandy, you didn't. You threatened him, yes. Would you have cut him? I don't know, but you *didn't*. You can't beat yourself up about this. Parents will do absolutely anything to protect their young, anything." Mike paused. "I know a thing or two about it, Sandy. My dad trained me to be the fighter of the pack. I'm not the Alpha but I'm the muscle. I'm expected to keep everyone safe, all the time. He turned me into this machine, and I don't even think about it anymore. I didn't think about it when I talked to Jacks about fighting, it's just all I know. And it makes this whole thing my fault, see? I made Jacks fight Sean in a way that would overpower and dominate him. It's not even the way regular kids fight, Sandy. I just don't know anything else. I'm stupid like that."

Sandy burrowed her head in deeper to his chest, curling her legs up beside her. "There's not anything stupid about you, mountain man, unless it's that you bought that horse-shit. You know I'd never love a moron. I mean, come on, you can do anything at all that you set your mind to. Your heart is the size of a..well, I guess, a Bear's heart, and you protect everyone around you, all the time. How can someone do that with no brain?" Sandy sighed. "They can't. You can't."

The phone rang, a phone left out on the counter. "Who's

phone is that?" Sandy asked. Mike was already moving to answer it. He listened silently and put it down.

"Kids!" Mike yelled up the stairs, and Cassy and Jacks poked their heads out of their rooms. "We got to go, right now, grab what you need and get down here."

They scrambled and Mike turned to Sandy. "I know they are yours, Sandy. I just... He's got Kurt, Sandy. My little brother. Travis, he wants us both there. I'd rather bring the kids than leave them here alone. My brothers are there; they can watch them. We have to go, now."

Sandy wiped her face and got the kids out the door. "Deal, Mike. We're all in it now. Okay? We're with you."

Mike drove Sandy's little car headlong across town and up into the hills.

nother semi-circle of Bears, plus one Wolf. Another mine shaft. Mike shook off the *déjà vu* and tried to focus on what he was seeing now. He knew this was different but all he could see was Kurt's crumpled form at the feet of the enormous black Wolf. Mike had shifted to Bear form when he got the guard settled in with the kids. Sandy was by his side. In fact, she was resting her hand on the scruff at the back of his head. He'd never had anyone touch him when he was in Bear form, and it was definitely not something he minded. Sandy seemed to be taking some comfort from it, so there was that.

Kurt let out a whimper, drawing Mike back to his laser focus. Sandy yelled out. "What do you want, Travis? What do you want from me? Why did you want me here? Please let Kurt go, he is hurt…let his brothers have him…"

Mike vaguely heard a 'tsk' sound from one of the other Bears and turned his head to look at Sandy.

"What?! You're all Bears! Unless you can talk, let me do the work here! I know how to talk to animals, Mike, remember!? I… I won't provoke him, unless I can get him away from

Kurt, so you can get to him, okay?" Sandy whispered in a fierce voice.

Mike lowered his head in acquiescence.

"Now, let me do this. Don't worry. Just…have my back, all right? I need you there."

Mike nodded again.

Sandy let go of his scruff and stepped forward.

"Travis? Is that you in there? I'm here now, I came when I got the call. Why did you want me here?"

The Wolf lowered his snout to look at her. Sandy took another step.

"Can you come forward a little? I can't really see your whole shape and I don't know Wolf language very well. I… Can you change back? I mean, you've still got the power of having Kurt in there, so the Bears won't attack, but I can't hear you or find out how to give you what you want if you stay like that." Sandy turned to the Bears. "Can I promise you won't attack if he changes? Can we make it fair somehow? So he'll change, and I can talk to him?"

The Bears looked at each other and the Bear she presumed was Bill nodded.

"Okay, Travis. They give their word they won't attack. Will you please shift? So I can talk to you? I'll come in the cave, yes."

At that, she heard multiple growls from behind her. She waved them down and fiercely whispered, "I can handle this. Stand down!"

She stepped forward again. She felt Mike take a step forward behind her and watched the Wolf bare his teeth and step back toward Kurt. "Stop!" She turned to Mike. "I have Bill's word. Stand by it. I can do this. Let me."

Mike put his head down. The other Bears looked at each other in what looked like shock. Sandy didn't know what was going on, but had to turn back to Travis.

"Okay, Travis. I will come halfway but I need you to shift so I know I can talk to you. I'm not coming in there with your Wolf."

Sandy had no idea what she was doing, really, but she knew how to talk to aggressive animals. As long as she kept her voice calm and her movements slow, she wasn't a threat, and wouldn't trigger an attack. Of course, the animals she knew were just animals, not crazy people. *Okay, get it together, Sandy. Just focus.* She stepped forward again, and waited.

She could see behind Travis now, into the shaft. She knew she didn't want to go in there, whether Travis was a man *or* a Wolf. It was dark, and too narrow. Travis was not to be trusted as a man, that much she knew. She just needed to get him away from Kurt so the Bears could do their thing.

She watched as Travis stepped forward, away from Kurt. She could see a shimmer above the Wolf's head and watched, mesmerized, as his black coloring faded and he shrank down to man-sized. Travis was naked and obviously proud of his naked form, as he gestured at himself once he changed.

"Like me now, Sandy?! You see what I can do, right? You uppity bitch." He came closer to her, step by step. Sandy backed up. "You want to know what I want? I want you down on your knees, begging me, that's what I want… I want to see you grovel, and I want Mike over there to be watching you grovel *to me.* I'll tell you where Cassy is once you do."

Sandy was shocked. *He thinks I'm doing this for Cassy. He doesn't know I've already got Cassy?!* Her brain reeled. *How is that possible? How could he not know?* Facts and possibilities rolled through her brain as she tried to accommodate the new situation. Travis had no idea the precariousness of his own situation. He still thought he had undeniable power over her. She had to keep him thinking that.

"Okay, Travis, Okay. Step out here, let's do it. You want everyone to see? Let's do it. I'll do anything you want, Travis,

I will." Sandy got down on her knees. She felt the earth shake with a deep Bear growl behind her but needed to keep going. She just needed him out of the cave, and exposed.

Travis stepped forward, full of swagger and bravado, naked or not.

I just need him a couple steps further.

"Here I am, Travis. Come make me beg. I'm such a bitch, right? I turned you down how many times? Here's your one and only shot, I'll beg for Cassy, I will. I love her more than anything. What do you want me to do for you, Travis?"

Sandy did everything she could to make it seem like she was offering Travis exactly what he wanted, audience or not. She could only hold her breath now, and hope he took the next two steps.

He did. Before he put his foot down on the second pace, he was facing a Bear paw. There were so many Bears in the mix, Sandy couldn't tell what was happening. But in less than a minute, it was over. Travis was on his back with some long red claw marks along his front. He was alive, but the Bear holding him down seemed almost protective.

Sandy looked up to see Mike, in man form, leaning over Kurt with a concerned look on his face. Kurt said something in reply, and Mike laughed and lightly cuffed him on the forehead. The look of relief on his face was evident.

Sandy sat back on the ground, a still center in a mass of action. She closed her eyes and felt Mike arrive at her side.

"You, you are the most amazing woman I have ever encountered. You just saved my baby brother, and faced down a crazy-ass shifter. I cannot even tell you how much I love you, Sandy. You are it for me, the only, forever. Please, tell me you forgive me."

Sandy opened her eyes. "Forgive you? Oh my god, Mike. You saved my children! I have never felt as safe as when I'm with you, there's no bravery when you're at my back, Mike.

It's certainty. I know there is nothing that will harm me. I love you like a crazy person, Mike, Bear or man or both, wildly and out of control. I do, I just completely do."

Mike held her in his arms while a swirl of Bears and men moved around them both, rounding up Travis and giving Kurt some well-needed medical attention.

Sandy laughed. "Um, are any of these men going to put on clothes, Mike? I mean, I'm sure this isn't how I'm supposed to get to know your family."

Mike laughed loudly. "Let's go get the kids, Sandy, and I'll get you away from all this nakedness. You can meet them more officially and more clothed tomorrow. It's time to go home. I'll give you some very specific nakedness to focus on later."

Sandy glanced down at him and giggled. "Hallelujah, Mike, hallelujah."

ike and Sandy were standing, looking at the front of the garage, holding hands. He'd been finishing the project on his own, bringing it up to code and not taking a dime of Sandy's money. He wanted so badly to give her something, to make all her dreams come true.

Sandy whispered, "I can't believe it's here, it's done. Jewel's Rescue is official now. I never could have done this without you, Mike. I am so thankful to Ruby." She sputtered out a guffaw.

Mike shook his head. "Oh, baby. I am so thankful to Ruby, too. She gave me the greatest love of my life, and I'm never going to lose it. I've been given a whole family, and I'm going to spend the rest of my days protecting and loving the woman in charge."

He leaned down to her. "I mean Ruby, of course." He sputtered out his own guffaw.

"Oh my god, again?" Cassy whined in sarcasm, "Jackson, can't you do something?" Cassy and Jackson were standing back looking at the garage as well.

A large new sign had been placed where a hoop had been. 'Jewel's Rescue', it said.

"Nah," said Jackson. "Let them have their moment, Cass. They deserve it."

Cassy and Jackson smiled and went inside.

There had been a few hitches to having Mike around but overall, the kids were thrilled. They'd never not-miss their Dad, but Mike was a safe and dependable and loving man, and they were growing to love him.

Mike watched them go. He turned and enveloped Sandy in a giant hug, lifting her off the ground. "I love your kids you know." He nuzzled his face in her hair. "But, more importantly than that, I was curious, little lady, if you'd like to celebrate on that bench in there? It's worked in the past, but you know, it's all new now... We definitely need to christen this whole operation, and there are very good locks on all the doors. I took care of that myself."

Sandy snickered. "Well, my mountain man, I never thought you'd ask!" She was happier than she had ever been. She couldn't believe that this was her life. After all this time of doing it all alone, she had a partner and a love. It was just absolutely perfect.

Mike carried her right into the garage, both of them laughing as they went. The doors closed behind them with a satisfying click.

***

Thanks so much for reading Enemy Daddy Bear! I hope you loved it! If you did then I'm pretty sure you will love another series we have, this one called the Bridge Hollow Shifters, from Samantha Leal...

Click here to read the Bridge Hollow Shifters Complete Collection, here on Amazon.

TROUBLE IS COMING TO BRIDGE HOLLOW - A STRANGE mountain town full of mystery...where nothing is as it seems...

WITH A SIX WEEK BREAK TO FILL AND PLENTY TO RUN FROM, timid teacher Amanda decides it's time to break the mold and go on a random road trip with her best friend to the mysterious town of Bridge Hollow.

BRIDGE HOLLOW IS FAMOUS FOR ITS STRANGE HAPPENINGS AND shifter legends, but skeptic Amanda just wants to chill out for the summer and catch her breath after a particularly rough breakup.

BUT OF COURSE ANYTHING SHE GETS INVOLVED IN IS BOUND TO be "complicated", and this town – and town alpha Dean - are no exception. From a wildlife die off to the volatile locals tempers flaring at the slightest provocation – there is definitely something strange going on in this paranormal tourist trap.

· · ·

As Dean pulls his pack together to avert a firestorm, will Amanda be his 'ace in the hole' or a weakness he can't afford?

Here is a brief preview of Alpha Daddy Bear, the first story in the Bridge Hollow series…

Bridge Hollow – Present Day

The woods were dark as the two men made their way across the bubbling stream. The rocks were slippery underfoot, the water flowing fast, and they steadied themselves against each other as to not to lose their footing.

"It's cold out here," David said as he stopped and exhaled. He couldn't fully tell with there being so little light, but he thought he may have seen a wisp of icy air clinging to his breath as he spoke, and it sent a chill right down his spine.

"I've never seen it like this," his companion, Ben, said as he stopped and hitched his gun up onto his broad shoulder. "Maybe that's why we're not getting much luck..." he clicked his teeth and sighed as he looked back down the stream, towards the folds of trees that were bending and dipping across them from overhead. The branches were thick and full of green, but even with that considered, these two hunters were used to this forest. They knew it like the back of their hands, and both could tell that there was something strange happening there around them.

This day, something was very, very different indeed.

"It's the middle of summer," David said. "This place should be crawling with deer."

Ben shrugged and reached into his back pocket for a pack of smokes. He clamped one between his teeth and reached for a lighter.

"Oh, that's a great idea," David snorted with a wry smile. "That'll really attract the animals."

Ben rolled his eyes and lit up anyway. He sucked in deeply and exhaled before he turned and climbed up and over the rocks, onto the muddy side of the embankment and out of the chill of the water.

"Thing's ain't been right round here for a while,' he said as he crouched down and ran his fingertips into the ground. The earth was threateningly cold, with a force he had never known before. It wasn't just the cool soil in the shadows, this was something deep from within. Something menacing and raw.

"This fucking town," he whispered. "If it's not crazed tourists flooding the streets looking for Bigfoot or whatever the hell they believe, it's the locals slowly going insane with the rumors and legends."

"Well maybe it's high time we stopped coming here then," David said goadingly. "But I think we all know what brings you to these parts. You can mock the tourists all you want, but what you're looking for is your own juicy piece of the pie."

The men looked at each other knowingly and Ben took one last drag before he stubbed out his cigarette on the base of his boot, threw the butt into the gush and pull of the stream and started to laugh.

"May as well," he winked as he let his rifle drop to the floor beside his feet and then he sat with his legs dangling over the ridge.

David climbed up beside him and the pair sat together looking around. For a summer's day the forest was bleak and freezing. It was not long past noon, and they were right to be wary. It was clear to them both, as seasoned hunters, that something was amiss out there.

"Do you think it's Bigfoot coming to get us?" David joked as he reached for his water bottle and took a long, deep sip.

"Don't be foolish," Ben replied. "It is something though, alright."

The sun was nowhere to be seen, but there didn't appear to be a cloud in the sky. The break in the trees above showed blue, but there was something strange about it. Something other-worldly. The air was still and chilly, like a veil had descended and trapped them there in their own little bubble.

"Come on," David got to his feet and stretched before he reached down and scooped up his rifle and slung it back over his shoulder. "We may as well get out of here. It's a lost cause. If we go fast we'll get the best part of the afternoon over in the bar instead, the wives don't need to know a thing."

Ben laughed and nodded. David helped him up and they began to walk further into the forest.

The men crunched over the earth and when Ben looked

down he was sure he saw a frost forming. As they got further into the trees and closer to the center which would allow them to cross back over to where they had parked on the outskirts, the woods got darker still and the air became prickly and vengeful.

Ben looked towards David and he could see his face darkening too. Neither of them spoke a word, but with each step forward they took, they were getting further and further away from the light, and further from the world they knew. They were descending into something unknown. Something dark and powerful. As they stepped through a thick section of trees and emerged into a clearing, Ben's breath caught in his throat and his whole body was shocked with cold. It pierced him deep within his heart and kept him there, paralysed with fear.

David stopped too, and Ben was aware of the rifle falling again. Down to the ground, crunching onto the frost under their feet and turning icy and white as it connected with the earth.

"My God," Ben gasped. His eyes widened as he took in the scene in front of him.

For a moment, he was sure that he must be dreaming. None of this could be real. He blinked and lifted his shaking hands towards his eyes where he tried to rub them, but the cold wouldn't allow his fingers to move. They were frozen in place, quickly turning red and frost bite taking hold.

"Dav...id..." his voice cracked. The cold travelled through his mouth and right down to the pit of his stomach. It gripped him like nothing he had ever known before and within a second it was as if he were turning to stone.

Before them both, as they stood there freezing, the last things their eyes saw was the scene in the forest.

The trees above them were turned brown and black, their trunks and roots poisoned from the ground up. A fog was heavy in the air, something dank and sweet, trails of energy wisping up from the cracks in the earth below. The circle in the center of the clearing. The darkness and the death. Heaps and heaps of bodies. Animals of the woods that had gathered there, in that very spot and met their end, just like Ben and David themselves. The circle of bears, wolves, deer, rabbits, racoons and birds were all piled together, in a swirling pattern, all facing the central point of the clearing.

It was like something out of a horror movie. Something unnatural, dark and magical. But not the good kind of magical. Something utterly terrifying. Whatever had come to the woods of Bridge Hollow had managed to kill off at least a hundred animals. Either they had been led to their death, or they had been called.

Now Ben and David were a part of them. They would never make it to the bar on Main Street, and they would never get to tell their wives what they had seen that day. They would certainly never hunt again.

Some would have said that was a good thing.

Some would think it terrible luck.

But for the animals of Bridge Hollow, it was only just the beginning. They may not have had Bigfoot lurking around them, but they sure as hell had something. And now it was coming out to play in full force.

The cold slowly began to lift, and the animals sank into the ground like it was quicksand, taking David and Ben along with them. Like the saying often went, the ground opened and swallowed them whole. Slowly and silently, one by one. Any evidence of what had occurred there was completely destroyed, taken away as if it had never happened at all.

The darkness lifted, but the chill remained.

The sun broke through the trees and lit up the clearing, the fog cleared, but the energy there would be forever changed. There was something magical about this place. Something deep and meaningful. Something that the locals were either going to have to embrace or fight.

Bridge Hollow was never going to be the same again...

You know you want to visit Bridge Hollow... a new town with new mysteries ...
...Get it here on Amazon ...;)

www.ingramcontent.com/pod-product-compliance
Lightning Source LLC
Chambersburg PA
CBHW052105150726
48002CB00006B/2221